THE FARMER'S WAR

ELISE KOVA

Silver Wing Press

THE FARMER'S WAR

ELISE KOVA

Silver Wing Press

Published by Silver Wing Press
Copyright © 2017 by Elise Kova

Cover Illustration by Merilliza Chan
Scene Illustration by Kolarp Em
Content Editing by Katie Ackley
Line Editing by Rebecca Faith Hayman

eISBN: 9781619846449
Paperback ISBN: 978-1619846432
Hardcover ISBN: 978-1619846425

2022 Five Year Anniversary Edition

ALSO BY ELISE KOVA

See the most up to date list of all of Elise's books, and find where to get them, on her website at:

https://elisekova.com/books/

AIR AWAKENS UNIVERSE

Readers can start with any series in the Air Awakens universe. Books in series should be read in order.

Golden Guard Trilogy

The Crown's Dog

The Prince's Rogue

The Farmer's War

Air Awakens Series

Air Awakens

Fire Falling

Earth's End

Water's Wrath

Crystal Crowned

Vortex Chronicles

Vortex Visions

Chosen Champion

Failed Future

Sovereign Sacrifice

Crystal Caged

A Trial of Sorcerers

A Trial of Sorcerers

A Hunt of Shadows

A Tournament of Crowns

(More to Come)

THE LOOM SAGA

The Alchemists of Loom

The Dragons of Nova

The Rebels of Gold

MARRIED TO MAGIC

A Deal with the Elf King

A Dance with the Fae Prince

A Duel with the Vampire Lord

(More to come)

for Dani
thank you for being in my "Golden Guard"

TABLE OF CONTENTS

Prologue 1
1. Craig 5
2. Daniel 15
3. Craig 23
4. Daniel 29
5. Craig 35
6. Daniel 41
7. Craig 49
8. Daniel 55
9. Craig 63
10. Daniel 71
11. Craig 77
12. Daniel 87
13. Craig 97
14. Daniel 101
15. Craig 105
16. Daniel 111
17. Craig 121
18. Daniel 129
19. Craig 133
20. Daniel 139
Epilogue 145

DISCOVER MORE FROM ELISE KOVA

Vortex Visions 153
A Trial of Sorcerers 155
Air Awakens 157

About the Author: Elise Kova 159

THE
MAIN CONTINENT
VANGAR
THE CRYSTAL CAVERNS
SOLARIN
"THE CAPITAL"
RIVEND
MOSA
THE GREAT IMPERIAL WA
OPARIUM
THE
SOUTH
LYNDUM
PACA
LEOUL
SHAN
THE FINSHAR DELTA
HAST
THE
EAS
CYVE

THE CRESCENT CONTINENT
THE BARRIER ISLANDS
THE WEST
MHASHAN
QUI
NORIN
XIA
LAU
SILME
YON
ORE
THE CROSSROADS
ANTO
POHEAT
THE PASS
DAMACIUM
SORICIUM
LAKE IO
THE NORTH
ALDA
SHALDAN

PROLOGUE

Daniel Taffl was never going to lie about directions ever again.

It wasn't that he'd wanted to lie, or had even intended not to tell the truth. It had just sort of come out that way. At worst, he anticipated an extra day added to his mission through the forest. As it turned out, the punishment for slanting the truth would be far more severe.

Stuck in a spiked pit in hostile territory with one of the most tiresome men he'd ever met, a giant angry cat prowling and growling from the only entry above, was a whole new level of wrong.

Daniel looked over at unconscious man lying across from him, propped against a boulder. Lieutenant Craig Youngly had been hand-picked by Major Raylynn Westwind to be her personal apprentice, yet still he claimed not to care about rank and file. Someone who had more power than most men could dream of, albeit by virtue of proximity to those more powerful even than himself, and he had no interest in honoring the hierarchy that set him apart. In living up to his claim, he had proven himself a most annoying sort.

Luckily, right now, the Lieutenant was passed out. Daniel found he preferred this version of the blonde-haired man, who in this state lacked the ability to tug on his very last nerve. Yes, the silent version of Lieutenant Craig was the best version.

Daniel's ire faded some as his eyes fell on Craig's haphazardly bandaged leg. Blood had already soaked through the cotton and puddled on the stones around his appendage. Daniel was no cleric, and his clumsy attempt at getting the wound on the mend had put the other man through enough trauma to knock him out.

It would have been a satisfying little victory in successfully shutting him up, were the situation not so grim.

He tilted his head back, watching stones and dirt crumble free from the opening and into the pit as the giant cat continued to pace—slower than before. Eventually, it would tire of the prey that eluded it. But even when it did, they would still be left with no food, minimal shelter, and the increasingly likely failure of their mission on behalf of the prince's Golden Guard.

Daniel closed his eyes and gave a long sigh, releasing his tension and ignoring the desire to sit back in frustration. There wasn't time for throwing up his hands and giving in. Even in the most dire situation, one could find opportunities with an open mind. If Daniel ever wanted to see his betrothed again, he needed to focus on getting out of this predicament alive.

His mind betrayed him with that brief thought. *Willow.* What was she doing now? All the woman had asked of him was that he fight and return home alive. Now, he was risking his life for the possibility of a more secure future in the form of Imperial favor and gold—gold beyond his soldier's pittance, and gold they didn't technically need.

Daniel wanted to make Willow proud. He wanted to keep safe. But he also wanted to do everything he could to succeed in a place where no one expected a farmer's son to survive even a single day.

Daniel's eyes opened anew, and his mind went to work.

1

CRAIG

ANY OF THE soldiers who thought him lucky for his closeness with Raylynn Westwind had very little idea of what the woman was actually like.

"You were so sloppy."

Sure, she had a song-like voice, lilting and deceptively easy on the ears. And fine—perhaps when she moved, it was with the intimidating grace of a dancer moving to the twin rhythms of death and seduction.

"I realize," Craig replied dryly.

"I mean, look at you." Raylynn drew a line through a splatter of blood that covered half his right arm. Her figure could make men weak in the knees even when she was fully clad in armor, a fact that was often reason enough to draw jealousy from other men… and women. "You're a mess."

"I realize," Craig repeated.

"I taught you better than this, you know," she said with a laugh that contrasted brightly against the haze of gore that hung heavy on the battlefield.

"I realize." It was automatic—*Let her talk it out. She'd exhaust herself eventually.*

"But there really is no helping you, is there?" Raylynn stopped at the field's edge. A shift in her demeanor signaled that Craig was no longer about to get the verbal lashing he'd been bracing himself for. "See that my tent is set up just there, and let the other lieutenants know we'll be camping here for the night. Find Jax, and tell him we need to regroup, count our losses."

The moment Raylynn wandered off to the next recipient of her reprimand, Craig executed her orders to the letter. First, he located the soldiers in charge of Raylynn's things. Then he found Jax among the other Firebearers—torching bodies and foliage alike.

"Well, if it isn't Raylynn's favorite toy come to call." The Western man didn't spare Craig so much as a glance. "To what do I owe this high esteem from her golden holiness?"

"If you know it's me without looking, maybe that same magic will tell you why I'm here." Craig crossed his arms, silently proud of himself for not being goaded into remarking on the man's "favorite toy" comment... *this time.*

"I assume she's settling in and wants to know the state of the Black Legion." Jax finally tore his eyes away from the pyre that had been working its way up a tall tree. Northern structures—glorious treetop cities—were reduced to ash and cinder by the blaze. Another city had been subsumed by the flames of war, and Craig had long since stopped feeling much at all over it.

It was not mere coincidence that the fire seemed to dim when the dark-haired man turned his way.

Jax was abrasive, downright mental, hilariously unhinged, and as a fallen lord, he had nothing left to lose.

Atop it all, he was one of the most powerful Firebearers Craig had ever laid eyes on. He didn't need to be a sorcerer to know that tumbling with the major would be akin to fiery suicide. The only man who could claim to be Jax's superior in magical skill would be the Fire Lord himself—the Crown Prince Aldrik.

"Well, let's go, little toy." Jax patted Craig on the head like a child. "If there's one thing you never do, it's keep a lady waiting. Especially *this* particular lady."

Craig grit his teeth and followed behind. His hands smoothed his hair back into place, blond strands ruffled more from the battle, he assured himself, than from Jax's interference.

"Took you long enough," Raylynn said dryly upon their entry to her tent.

Knowing he wasn't the one being addressed, Craig stepped to the side of the canvas-walled abode, closer to Raylynn than Jax. The two majors held equal commissions in the army, the golden bracers on their forearms elevating them to a league above the rest. The only reason Craig could even stand among them as anything resembling an equal was a direct result of Raylynn's favor for him.

"Bodies don't burn themselves." Jax shrugged then stilled. "Though, it'd be mighty convenient if they did... Could you imagine? A man gets cut down, his heart stops beating, and then boom! A self-cleaning battlefield. Just fires left and right—"

Raylynn held up a hand, stopping the Firebearer's pyromantic fantasies. "The Legion?"

"The Black Legion holds strong. Only a handful of casualties."

Craig had to focus on keeping his mouth still so he didn't

mirror the Western man's words right along with him. Seven battles, two cities and three outposts conquered since they left Soricium, and the report from the Black Legion was the same every time: a handful of casualties and overall strength. This was the might of sorcerers. A single member of the Black Legion could stand against three regular infantry. It was becoming expected—this report, the major's words. Commonplace, even.

The world was lucky that those with magic were genetically outnumbered at least five to one. If not, sorcerers could very well be running things, and everyone knew that would lead to ruin. All one had to do was look at the War of the Crystal Caverns for proof.

"At least *someone* on the field was competent today." Raylynn cast a sideways look at Craig.

"Oh-ho, what's this? Lover's quarrel?" Jax hummed and hawed. The look on his face was bordering on lewd, and it took all Craig had not to roll his eyes in distaste.

"He'll have to become far more competent in battle before I consider taking him to bed." Raylynn laughed at the notion; while he hardly thought of her as a potential conquest, he felt defensiveness rise involuntarily.

"The lady made no complaints after our last skirmish," Craig reminded her, not without a silent flicker of pride. The fearlessness still surprised even himself.

"He grows bold!" Jax clapped his hands with a wide grin. "Maybe there's hope for him yet, Ray."

"He certainly wants us to think so."

"You still chasing after one of these?" Capturing Craig's eye with a teasing smirk, Jax held up his arm. Strapped around it was the most beautiful thing Craig had ever laid his eyes on: a golden bracer. Craig schooled his features before answering.

"I know they can only be offered by one man."

"That's a yes, then." Jax leaned against Raylynn's table nonchalantly. "You know, I have an idea for you, Craig. If you do something for me, I'll put in a good word for you with the prince."

Anything that seemed too good to be true usually was—especially when it came to Major Jax Wendyll. Craig remembered the last time Jax had offered him a "promotion". It came with six weeks of overseeing latrines. "What's the catch?"

"No catch. Do something for me, and I'll do something for you. Simple."

"What do you want me to do?" Craig was wary, but cautiously optimistic. A year and a half was enough time to earn someone's trust. And it had been at least that long since Raylynn had taken him on as her sort-of page, student, apprentice, steward… whatever their relationship was.

"Something simple." Jax glanced at the table. "Like, delivering a letter to Baldair."

"You want me to deliver a letter?" Craig couldn't help but feel the man was making up the whole idea second to second, and Jax did nothing to dissuade this notion. In fact, he seemed perfectly serious.

"Yes, I want you to deliver a letter to the prince. Oh, and it'll actually be of the utmost importance." Jax rounded the table to where Raylynn stood, lifting one of her quills and commandeering some of her parchment.

"I don't think you've done anything of importance in your life, Jax," she said under her breath.

Jax responded with an overdramatic gasp. "You wound me, fair lady! And here I thought we were friends."

Raylynn snorted and continued laying out tokens on the map, cross-referencing reports and updates she'd gathered from the other lieutenants on their forces. "We're not very much friends if you take away the best sword I have."

In the wake of genuine surprise, Craig's chest swelled with pride. There might be hope for him yet apparently, even after his "sorry" performance on the field.

"If he's the best sword you have, you really are carrying things on the front line by yourself." Jax folded the parchment he'd scribbled on before Craig had a chance to glance at its contents. He broke off a piece of sealing wax, placing it in the center of the paper and pressing his thumb into it. The wax melted by magic, leaving the indent of his finger as he pulled it away.

"Showoff." Raylynn yawned for emphasis of how impressed she wasn't.

"I am just the best, aren't I?" Jax grinned wildly at Raylynn before handing the letter to Craig. "Get that to the prince in less than ten days, and you'll have my vote of confidence to wear a bracer."

"You're really doing this?" Raylynn sighed, finally pulling up her eyes from the documents. "We sort of need him here... you know... for the actual war."

"We'll be fine. You can fight circles around him anyway, right?" Raylynn didn't object to Jax's assessment and Craig kept his mouth shut. It wasn't even an affront to his pride; Raylynn could fight circles around anyone in the army who could hold a sword. With the exception of, perhaps, Prince Baldair. "You can always find a new pet, Ray."

Craig cringed. Raylynn sighed.

"Don't you have someone in mind?" Jax nudged the woman. "Exchange this one for a new, young swordsman with actual talent? Perhaps even find one this time who's gifted in bed?"

In a way that only Jax could, he struck a chord with Craig's personal… accomplishments. Even if he put his ego aside and looked at it objectively, Craig had never heard a word of complaint from any woman he'd *entertained*. If he hadn't been worried of the potential fallout, and if she'd expressed even a passing interest, Craig would've shown Raylynn Westwind just how good he could be. Any man with eyes would do the same.

"I doubt the one I have in mind would be any more gifted."

The realization hit Craig with sobering clarity. *She has someone else in mind.*

"I hear he has a betrothed waiting for him back in the Capital. Sentiment distracts men and makes them too eager for heroics or too cowardly in the name of self-preservation."

A betrothed. Craig began to mentally list off soldiers he knew to be engaged, unconsciously comparing himself—his swordsmanship, of course—to each.

"So a sword of a different nature has caught your eye," Jax carried on as if Craig had vanished long ago.

But Craig hadn't disappeared. He was still very much engaged in the banter, and the twin task of narrowing the list of his potential replacements at Raylynn's side. He'd been studying under the woman for nearly two years and they'd been through over thirty battles together. He wasn't about to lose his place to some upstart.

But he also wasn't about to lose his chance at a golden bracer.

"… it's not a standard issue blade," Raylynn continued.

All at once, he knew the identity of his would-be replacement. His fist tightened around the piece of parchment in his palm, mind formulating a quick and precise plan of attack. "Major Jax, I will deliver your letter."

Jax blinked, glancing in Craig's direction. "Oh, you're still here?" The Western man seemed genuinely surprised. "Or have you gone and returned already?"

"I will be back before you even realize I'm gone." Craig gave his strategy one last mental review before launching into it with confidence and persistence. "But seeing as I am to trek through dangerous territories, I think it best if I have a partner."

"Can't handle it?" Jax raised his eyebrows, half mocking and half weighing Craig's valor. "Not very Golden Guard-like of you. If we can't trust you to deliver a letter, then—"

"You can trust me. I'm assuring the letter's delivery." Craig tried to think quickly without backpedaling. "If I fall, I'll have a second to carry the mission forward." Jax didn't look entirely convinced, but he also didn't comment further, leaving Raylynn to chime in on the matter.

"Who did you have in mind?" It was obvious she was already way ahead of him. She had been the whole time, the tiniest of teasing smiles playing across her lips.

"Daniel Taffl."

Craig didn't know much about the Easterner, but was sure of two facts above all: Daniel spoke regularly of the "love of his life" back in the Southern Capital, and he had a custom-forged rapier that could turn even Raylynn's head.

Raylynn was one for constant tests—mental war games

to keep Craig on his toes—and this time, her growing smile suggested he'd passed this one with flying colors. "Very well. Have this Daniel fellow brought here to join you on Jax's twisted little quest." She dismissed him with a wave of her hand, pretending as though she'd never heard the name before.

2

DANIEL

S TRIPPING THE DEAD was his least favorite task.

He felt like a beetle in a wheat field. But instead of golden stalks towering over him, thick trunks—larger than six grown men could reach around by touching fingertips—spread a dense canopy of foliage across the sky. Daniel squinted at the swaying leaves high above, wondering if death still lurked among them in the form of the Empire's only remaining enemies on the main continent: Northerners. Unfortunately, the shifting viridian above him was not one to give up its secrets so easily.

It never did.

"Daniel, stop lollygagging!"

He snapped back to attention, his mind pulled back to the carnage before him and away from thoughts of wind and ruffled tufts of wheat before the summer harvest. He bent over once more, flipping a fallen woman onto her back. Daniel made a quick assessment of what was still salvageable. A buckler, a sheathe without its sword, shoes only half-worn through the soles... and nothing else.

Not even her name would be worth saving. There was barely enough time to search for reusable supplies. Whatever her name had been, it would be burnt along with the rest of her, lost to the large pyres that poured dark towers of smoke into the sky above the battlefield.

The dead woman would be kindling for the flames that would snake up those same trunks he had just caught himself admiring, tendrils weaving like vines into the branches above. Firebearers would stoke the flames to white, hot enough to peel away the bark thick and strong enough to be used as armor. Nothing would be left of this outpost, or its resistance against the Empire—nothing but scorched earth.

Once he'd collected all the macabre bounty his arms could carry, Daniel walked over to the men and women now sorting through leftover effects from the dead, making sense of the battalion's new influx of supplies.

"How much is left in the field?" a man asked.

"I think it's mostly done." Daniel wiped his brow with the back of his hand, squinting through smoke and heat distortion onto the field.

"Heard you weren't half bad out there."

Daniel gripped the pommel of his sword at the words. Pride swelled in his chest, curling around purpose. "I am merely serving the Empire."

"Aren't we all?" the man snorted, dropping whatever he'd been cataloguing into a pile before resting back on his thighs. "A soldier's wages are nothing to sniff at either."

"No, they're not." A soldier's compensation could be enough to buy a home, a respectable one with land that could be worked for generations to come. That or a modest abode in the city—if Willow's preference remained unchanged. That was assuming he survived long enough to see final installments of the payment he was owed.

"Daniel?" His name echoed across the field, broadcast from two hands cupped around a woman's mouth. "Daniel Taffl?"

He recognized the woman as another in his company, Ingrid. "I'm here!"

Ingrid crossed the distance to him in a hasty jog. A bandage clung tightly to her arm, weeping blood. The corners of his mouth tugged downward into the shape of a frown. The wound was on her sword arm.

"I see you made it through just fine," she said after a hasty assessment. He made sure not to let the flash of pity from earlier show on his face.

"I was lucky."

"There's a point at which luck is merely a synonym for skill. You'll have to admit it eventually."

Daniel ran his fingers over the pommel of his sword. Some of the men in his company had little issue with making their opinions on the thin rapier known. "A woman's blade," they'd called it. Two of the men who had made such arrogant remarks were no longer able to speak at all—unless the dead found voice roaming the Father's halls in the afterlife.

"A bit of both, I think." Pride was unbecoming at best, and at worst, begged for whatever luck he'd garnered to eventually run out.

"You've been requested in the Major's tent." At the mention of their superior, the small talk instantly ceased.

"I see."

Daniel couldn't imagine why Major Raylynn would be seeking him out, and likewise knew Ingrid had no more information to share. He followed behind her through the spotted carnage, remnants of North and South alike in the pitted mud of the forest floor. He kept his questions to himself, as a good soldier should. Following orders generally kept him alive, and those who gave them did nothing but command respect.

Few commanded more respect than Major Raylynn.

Her tent was erected on the edge of the opposite end of the field. Many-posted, it towered as the largest structure he'd seen in weeks. The interior bordered on luxurious for a soldier at war: a proper cot of canvas hung suspended above the rooted ground, and a table stood centrally—a place to conduct business and lay plans against their stubborn foes.

Behind that table was the woman in question.

"This is him?" Raylynn inspected Daniel the moment he entered. Ingrid nodded. "Good. You are dismissed, Ingrid." Ingrid retreated without another word, leaving him to the major's command. If he were a joking man, Daniel might even say he was at her mercy. Thankfully, he was more soldier than fool.

"Daniel Taffl, reporting for duty, major." He brought a fist to his heart in a practiced salute.

Her eyes scanned him from head to toe, landing for a long moment on the pommel of his sword. Daniel kept his focus on her, ignoring the other two men who occupied the tent. He knew there was only one opportunity to make a first impression, and he would not sully it with the carelessness of distraction.

"You have an interesting blade. Not standard issue." The major rounded the table, giving a small toss to her hair. Some of the soldiers called her the Golden Prince's sunbeam, noting the youngest Imperial prince's favor for her and her tresses of Southern blond. But Daniel never shared in such monikers. He had witnessed what this woman could do with a blade. She deserved far better than to be known only for her closeness to the prince. She was a blazing sun in her own right. Raylynn tilted her head as if reading his thoughts, eyes drifting lazily from sword to gaze. "Might I see it?"

It was phrased as a question, but Daniel knew he had no choice in the matter, not if he had any hope of keeping any standing in the army. He acquiesced and drew the weapon, holding it parallel to the ground for her assessment.

Raylynn waited until the blade stopped its quiet hum before taking it into her hands. *Beautiful and deadly*, they called her. Daniel had never refuted the assessment, but could see the resonant truth of it up-close. She was beautiful enough to be a lord's wife, even with—and perhaps especially because of—the scars that lined her body from head to toe.

Daniel didn't like letting others hold his blade—no true swordsman did—but there was something inherently different about the major that took some of the sting out of it. She seemed to know the weapon from the moment it touched her fingers. Daniel remained at ease through the inspection; there was no possibility the blade would fail under her scrutiny. It was one of the few things in his life he'd spent real money on, and it had taken one of the best smiths in Lyndum three weeks to forge.

"It's well made. An interesting choice for an Easterner."

Daniel ran a self-conscious hand through his telltale chestnut hair, though his Cyvense accent no doubt gave him wholly away. "My first swords were reeds from the riverbank by my father's fields as a child," he offered by way of explanation. Most Easterners found themselves in the pole-arm units, familiar primarily with pitchforks and sickles. "A weapon of this shape feels most natural."

"The steel agrees with your assessment."

It was a cryptic statement, and one Daniel didn't know how to reply to, so he said nothing. She could say whatever she wanted with her skill and the favor of the prince to back up her words. At least, for now, those words seemed in his favor.

"I can spare him for your task, Jax." Raylynn returned to her place at the table, aiming a small grin at the Western man who had been hovering at Daniel's right.

Jax. Major of the Black Legion—sorcerers—and another unconventional favorite of Prince Baldair. The gleaming metal bracer he and the major wore were useless as armor and unbecoming as jewelry, but were critically important nonetheless. That bracer signified the highest honor any soldier could ever hope to see: membership in the most elite fighting group, hand-picked by Prince Baldair himself, the Golden Guard.

"You're just too good to me." Jax's features hummed with the sort of look that, when turned Daniel's way, sent a flock of nerves up his spine and into the back of his mind, setting off a quiet alarm. But Daniel was trained to stay at attention, impassive and ready for orders. While all sorts of grim rumors surrounded the fallen lord—known to some as the Crown's Dog—he was still a Major and beyond that, another person whom Prince Baldair had deemed worthy to keep close. He was Daniel's superior in a multitude of ways, a fact that showed in the major's eyes when he finally said, "I have a task for you."

"For me?"

"You and Craig here will be delivering a letter for me, to Prince Baldair back in Soricum."

Daniel glanced at the man standing a half-step behind Jax. Another Southerner, judging from his striking blue eyes and golden hair.

"Shouldn't be an issue." The path they'd cut from Soricium would still be mostly cleared, Daniel reasoned, his thoughts already on the task at hand.

"It's a very important missive, and time is of the essence." The major's grin only continued to widen and Daniel could've sworn he heard a snort from Raylynn's side of the table.

"Then we shouldn't delay." *No questions*, Daniel reminded himself. He was a diligent soldier and he was in the North for a reason—to make his money and return home to build a life for him and Willow. She was waiting for him, counting on him to live up to his side of the arrangement.

"No, we shouldn't," Craig agreed. "I've secured two horses for us." The tone of his voice held a weight Daniel was unable to define, but it was easy to ignore in the face of their orders.

"Don't get yourselves killed," Major Raylynn muttered, engaged in moving tokens across her maps and cross-referencing a variety of notes.

"Or do, and make sure it's in such a horrible way that it becomes a tale to sing songs about," Major Jax added eagerly as the tent flap closed behind them.

A moment passed between the two soldiers. They were silent, their eyes pinned on the sealed entrance to Major Raylynn's tent. Craig was the first to break the quiet tension.

"Between the two, I'll take the former," he remarked dryly.

"Me as well." Daniel nodded before holding out his hand in greeting. "Daniel Taffl."

"Craig Youngly." The other man clasped his forearm firmly. "Shall we get this over with, Daniel?"

Daniel voiced his agreement earnestly. After all, it wasn't every day that one was called to task for a prince.

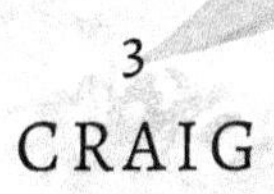

3

CRAIG

THE MEN AND women who served in the legions under Majors Raylynn and Jax had been marching for four weeks to the southwest of Soricium, a sort of zig-zag pattern to root out further resistance and lay waste to strongholds. But that time had been rife with stops for battles and burnings. Judging from Raylynn's map, Craig suspected they were only a ten day's ride from the capital of the North. That meant he should be able to cross the ground in six if they rode hard, thus completing their task well within the ten-day term Jax had set.

Six days, and he'd have two of the three Golden Guard members voicing their support of him to Prince Baldair. Six days, and he'd be that much closer to a golden bracer of his own. Craig could tolerate almost anything for six days. He'd been at war for two years now and had seen a wide range of conditions in that time, from the rainy months when soldiers began to rot alive from the damp, to weeks of living underground, waiting for the enemy to move. It was rare that he found something outright intolerable.

Which made the man at his side even more utterly insufferable.

"You seem chipper," Craig said, when he could hold in comment no longer.

"Pardon?" The look of confusion that overtook the man's face was a refreshing variation from the unnecessary cheerfulness he'd worn like a mask before.

"You haven't stopped smiling since we spurred off. Is scouting through enemy territory that much fun to you?" He traded his reins from left hand to right and gave a yawn to punctuate the thought.

"I have—"

"And the *whistling*." Like a dam bursting, the roster of annoyances began to flow freely from his mouth; the farther they got from camp, the less Craig was inclined to tolerate them.

"A habit I need to break." At least Daniel had the decency to look guilty for it. *What does Raylynn see in this man?*

"Without doubt. Surprised it hasn't gotten you killed yet." Craig glanced upward, an instinct they all had from being in the jungle too long. *Death comes from above.* It had only taken one ambush of Groundbreakers from the trees overhead for Craig to learn the truth first-hand. "You're as fresh as they come. Letting everyone within earshot know of your exact location? Might as well be shouting for the Northerners to come and pick you off."

"Right, lieutenant." Daniel pressed his lips together. Craig had no doubt that the flimsy physical reminder not to talk back would be as temporary as it looked.

"You can drop that nonsense." Craig waved a hand through the sunbeams that poked holes in the thick canopy dotting the sky—rare tracts of light determined to make it from the Mother's hand to the forest floor below. "No one out here wants it."

"But—"

"It just makes you seem greener than you already do, Daniel."

"Right. just Craig, then." Daniel adjusted his seat in the saddle. Even from the periphery, Craig could tell the order made the man uncomfortable. His companion was a solider through and through, wound tight by protocol and respect for the chain of command. It should have made Craig feel smug, superior even, but instead it just annoyed him further. And if he was being honest, chastened him a bit.

"Just Craig." He finally let out the frustrations he'd been holding in with a sigh. Everyone was this new at some point —that much he understood—but this soldier practically glowed green. A Golden Guard member must be patient with all soldiers, regardless of experience. He would embody what he aspired to be, no matter how difficult. "That won't be a problem, will it?"

"No, of course not." Daniel shifted in his seat again.

"Why does it make you so uncomfortable?"

"I…" His voice trailed off. Clearly, he hadn't given much thought himself to why the idea of not calling someone by proper rank and title bothered him so. "I want to make sure I'm giving you the proper respect." It was almost comical, the man's seriousness in the face of an uncommon situation. Greener and greener by the minute.

"Look, Daniel, can I give you a bit of advice?" When Daniel only proceeded to stare ahead in silence, back rigid with tension, Craig took it as permission to continue. "The titles and fanfare are left in the palace halls and city walls. On the field, the only respect that matters is doing as you're told. Save your ass and the asses of those around you, and it will surely be reciprocated."

"But—"

"Plus," Craig barreled forward. "Titles? Unnecessary protocols? They do little more than distance one soldier from another. When you more like another rank and file than a man's brother, it hinders the likelihood of him risking his neck for you."

For a long moment, Daniel remained silent, letting Craig's words resonate.

"I see," he said eventually, seeming to give the matter real thought. Craig hummed softly in approval; perhaps there was hope for him yet. Of course, Daniel opened his mouth shortly thereafter in what might have been the explicit intent of proving him wrong. "I must respectfully disagree, lieutenant."

The word "lieutenant" had never rankled him so badly. This Easterner had a real knack for finding new nerves to tug on.

"Because even out here, hierarchy is important. It is that fact more than any other that keeps soldiers doing as they're told."

Mother, this man was a toddler of a soldier. "What keeps men doing as they're told is the knowledge that the people giving the orders have a far better idea of what's going to keep them alive. It's all about self-preservation."

"It's about loyalty to the Solaris Empire."

"You are not under some kind of test." Craig rolled his eyes so dramatically his head turned with them. "Seriously, Daniel, this is going to be a long trip if you don't drop this 'good little soldier boy' bit and relax."

"I *am* relaxed," he huffed, though he contradicted the

statement nearly immediately by adjusting his position in the saddle for the third time. And then, for good measure, he added a terse "Lieutenant."

Call me lieutenant one more time, Craig wanted to say. Nearly did. Instead, he took a breath and replied with a strained, "Glad to hear it, *soldier*. Because we're in for a long trek back to the Northern capital."

Daniel said nothing, and in the nearly oppressive silence that followed, Craig realized he'd found the one thing they could both agree upon: It was going to be a very, *very* long few days.

4

DANIEL

HE WAS ON a mission for the prince. *The prince*. Of all the things Daniel expected to be doing when he marched off to war, taking on secret missions for one of the princes wasn't even in his wildest imaginings.

Then again…

It was the sort of fantasy he'd shared with Willow, their faces sharing two halves of the same pillow, in the nights leading up to his deployment. Every soldier dreamed of fanfare and glory, she'd assured him. All she wanted was for him to come home alive—a singular request that echoed in his mind every time he drew his sword.

But Daniel had always strived to do more than simply survive. He had assumed this risk for them both; by taking on a few more, he might be able to secure an even better future than they'd hoped. Surely, in the face of a royal errand's completion, the prince would offer some reward for a job well done?

He shifted in his saddle, stretching out the discomfort in

his thighs. It had been a long time since he'd merited a horse of his own, and it made traversing the gnarled , bramble-thick ground of the jungle far more bearable than trudging through on foot. Holding the reins again came naturally to him, even if his body was a bit out of practice. There had always been a horse on the farm for the plow, and certain livelihoods were hard to forget.

They'd ridden all day, and twilight was descending upon the world, blackening the canopy above. The shadows, their only company throughout the hours, began to creep out from their dens underneath the brush, claiming the world for darkness.

"We should make camp," Craig announced suddenly, his voice almost abrasive in the aftermath of such constant quiet. "There's no point risking our necks by marching through the night."

"Heard, lieutenant."

Craig's reins squeaked under his tightening grip as he led them toward a sapling of one of the great Northern trees. Daniel knew he'd earned Craig's ire yet again—and again for no good reason—so he decided to try for some friendly conversation.

"Still not used to them."

A pause. And then—

"Used to what?"

"The trees." Daniel tilted his head toward the shaded sentries that had hovered above them all day. "Even the little ones are taller than the pines in the Southern forests."

"You'll grow tired of them soon enough." The response seemed a bit clipped, but not unkind, which seemed an improvement over their previous exchanges. Daniel took it as a win, and watched as the other man dismounted, looping his horse's reins haphazardly over a branch. Daniel followed suit, trusting the mounts not to wander away.

"I'm not sure it will," Daniel hummed. "It hasn't happened yet…" He began unstrapping his bedroll from the back of his saddle. Even faced away, Daniel could practically hear the look of superiority on Craig's face.

"You're still green."

"I'm not *that* green," Daniel insisted defensively. Despite himself, he finished with a hastily murmured, "Sir."

"And there it is," Craig huffed, voice thick with smug teasing. "Couldn't resist your precious protocols after all, could you?" His tone softened a bit but remained no less annoyed. "I told you, none of that."

Craig tossed his own bedroll onto the leafy ground. The forest floor underneath the sapling was peaty. They'd wake up cold and damp, but better rested than on dryer locations with hard roots. There was no such thing as comfort in the jungle; it was just a matter of determining what discomfort was tolerable.

This time, the silence between the two men was far from companionable, filled with a tension Daniel was determined to break.

"I fear we may have gotten off on the wrong footing." He sat heavily on his makeshift bed, savoring what would likely be the only dry warmth he'd get all night. "I want you to know that I am taking this mission very seriously, and deeply respect your caliber as a soldier."

"Do you ever say anything authentic?"

The words twisted in Daniel's gut, raising his hackles instantly.

"Excuse me?"

"Wrong footing… mission… lieutenant… it's as if all you know how to say is what you think people want to hear." Craig shifted lazily, resting his chin in his palm. Unimpressed.

"I speak how I want to speak." It was clear his efforts to endear himself to the lieutenant were quickly turning south, evidenced by Craig's eye-rolling and audible scoffing.

"Right, and I'm the long-lost third prince Solaris."

"Far be it from me to comment on your lineage."

"That was remarkably close to a joke." Craig laid back onto his bedroll. "You'll ruin your image if you keep that up."

"It's not an image!" Daniel didn't know how else to convey the fact. He spoke how he wanted to speak and did what he wanted to do. Why was the man so determined to undermine him? What had he done to merit such blatant attacks on his character? The next words seemed to crawl up his throat unannounced. "*My* parents raised me right."

"And *that* was remarkably close to being rude. The 'good little soldier boy' cracks by the minute." Daniel didn't have to see Craig's face to know he was grinning with every word.

"We have a lot of ground to cover." Daniel peeled back the flap of his bedroll, wiggling into the inviting space within. The ground was soft and the wool still dry and warm. His muscles relaxed more than they had in weeks. "We should get some rest."

"And now he's giving *me* orders." Craig yawned loudly to punctuate the statement. "I don't remember getting word of your promotion."

Daniel pursed his lips. He wouldn't be egged into another round of verbal sparring. So he kept jaw clenched, lips pressed shut, until sleep settled over him, heavier than the blanket and heavier still than the fear of death in the night. The grim and determined line of his mouth persisted into the dawn.

5

CRAIG

THERE WAS SPORT in riling up his tightly-wound comrade. If he wasn't going to get good company out of the man, the least he could get was entertainment. And Daniel didn't disappoint.

Craig's joints popped and cracked in protest to the sleeping arrangements, a little chorus that sung for the dawn every day. He couldn't recall what it was like to sleep in a bed any longer. But all the pain and discomfort would be worth it in the end.

Deliver the letter. Get Jax's support. Continue to impress Raylynn. Don't disappoint Erion in any way. If he was lucky, he'd do something to impress Baldair himself.

The golden bracer was as good as his.

Daniel said nothing as they saddled up and set back on their course. Craig couldn't be sure if it was the result of his companion's obsession with hierarchy—Mother forbid he speak before being addressed by a superior—or if he was merely being stubborn, but Daniel's silence spread over the morning like dew. So Craig stayed equally as silent. If Daniel wanted to have conversation, he could be the first to broker one.

Even pettiness could be amusing, Craig decided. Considering there were so few genuine amusements at war, he reveled in his own.

The silence persisted until midday. By the time Daniel spoke, the stillness was all but ringing in Craig's ears.

"This looks strange…" he murmured, so softly that Craig was almost uncertain if he'd said anything at all.

"What does?" He decided to bite, perhaps a bit eager for a change in sound beyond the crunch of their horses' hooves against the forest floor.

"This tract of land…" Daniel swiveled in his saddle. His eyes darted up to the treetops above, scanning the flashes of light that poked through the canopy. "I don't remember it from the course here."

"It all looks the same." Craig shrugged, but obliged the other man by pulling out his compass. He'd at least make a show of needing to look at the navigation tool, even if his mind had already settled on the best heading. "One tree is almost impossible to tell from another."

"No, this is more than that."

"Compass says we're still on the right heading." Craig tapped the glass to ensure the needle wasn't stuck. It wasn't. "Due east. Soon enough we'll come across the charred remains of Tor, and then—"

"Lieutenant, with all due respect," Daniel interrupted, and Craig couldn't help but hear the irony in his tone. "I don't think we need to head completely east."

"Pardon?" Craig put away the compass, surprise slowing his motions. It was a very forward thing to say for the man who seemed wholly focused on following a soldier's protocol to the letter.

"We proceeded slightly south from Tor. I'd noticed from the sunrise through the canopy." Daniel stretched his legs in his saddle, avoiding eye contact. Craig blinked, looking from Daniel to the treetops and back.

"You couldn't possibly have seen the sunrise. You can't see anything through the canopy." He motioned upward for effect. Even now, the dense foliage could fool a man into thinking it was nearly night.

Daniel refused to look at him, back ramrod straight and jaw set. "You can see where first light breaks," he insisted.

With a heavy sigh, Craig ran a hand through his hair. This man *would* be the type to rise with the dawn, no doubt running every drill he could conceive. He likely had a fire started before a Firebearer could blink, food already cooked for his whole camp.

Craig knew full well he could simply order them forward on the course he knew to be correct; the Easterner wouldn't say anything if it was an order. But that would require Craig to pull rank. An invisible centipede crawled up Craig's spine at the thought. It would simply be justification for Daniel's ridiculous adhesion to the order of things.

He paused, glancing at the man out of the corner of his eye. *Had the bastard planned this?*

Craig pulled on his reins, punctuating the thought with a small grunt of frustration. Maybe this do-gooder was more manipulative than Craig had previously given him credit for.

He felt Daniel watching him as he rummaged through his saddlebags. There was a map Raylynn had quickly sketched for him folded up somewhere. It probably would have been wise to put it with the letter, strapped tightly to his hip for safe-keeping, but Craig hadn't foreseen himself needing it. The directions had been undeniably clear: Go east.

Map in hand, he scooped up the compass and squeezed his thighs against the sides of the saddle, using his knees to guide his horse over to Daniel. Once he was within range, he thrust map and compass directly into Daniel's chest.

"Right, then. If you're so apt with navigation, you can lead us."

"Sir?" The man didn't even move to take the two articles as he looked on in confusion.

"You seem to know where we should go..." Craig extended his arm just a little more, emphasizing that he wasn't about to let Daniel off the hook. "So why don't you lead?"

The other man's hazel eyes alternated between examining Craig's face and looking hesitantly at the offered map and compass. Finally, he reached out and snatched the items away with purpose.

"If you insist, sir."

"Oh, I do." Craig had never been more satisfied. At worst, Daniel would tack on an extra day with his insistence to go a little further north before cutting east. It was worth it to teach the man a lesson. "Take point, soldier."

Daniel held out the map in front of him with a slight squint. After some finger-pointing and squinting, he clicked his tongue, spurring his horse to action with a shift of his legs. Craig watched closely as Daniel took a slight lead ahead of him. For a foot-soldier he was fairly confident on a horse, Craig noted with interest—and vastly different from the fidgeting, constantly shifting rider he'd witnessed the day prior. Was Daniel hiding things from him?

"You sure you know where we're going?" Craig gave him one last chance as he glanced up at the canopy above, wondering how anyone could really see enough sunlight to know what direction they were facing. Daniel seemed determined though, voice insistent and confident.

"Of course I do. I have an excellent sense of direction."

6

DANIEL

D ANIEL DID NOT have an excellent sense of direction.

There were a good handful of feathers he could put in his cap, certainly. He could clear an entire field of barley in an afternoon. In the span of a few chirps, he could rough out the sketch of a bird he'd never seen before, capturing its likeness before it could fly off again. And above all else, he could use a sword with surprising precision and deadly efficiency. But directional prowess had never been one of his strong suits.

He still couldn't fathom what exactly had driven him to insist otherwise. He was lying, full stop, and lying to a direct superior at that. It was awful on every conceivable level and was made worse with each moment he refused to come clean.

Daniel shook his head, glancing back down at the map.

In truth, he *had* been paying close attention to the direction they'd been marching. Craig was right—it wasn't a hard course to chart. There was a chance Daniel was actually correct about them being slightly further south from the Imperial stronghold at the Northern capital. If so, he'd save face and a day of travel. He just had to have faith in his own abilities.

The bark of every surrounding tree seemed sculpted into judgmental faces, watching and waiting for the moment Daniel would confess the truth. Well, they could just keep on watching. He could fell a man in battle without blinking; he was hardly going to succumb to a couple of *trees*.

"Who made this map?" Daniel asked for some unfathomable reason. If he'd learned anything by now, it was not to expect any sort of conversation with his mission's comrade. Outside of clearing the air with a confession, which he had little desire to do, Daniel saw no reason to open his mouth at all.

As if in silent agreement, Craig spared Daniel not even a glance as he answered.

"Raylynn."

Against his better judgment, Daniel pressed. "I didn't realize the Major was such an accomplished cartographer." This elicited a sharp click of the tongue from the lieutenant.

"She's not and you know it."

Daniel didn't think it possible that someone could convey such utter disgust with a shake of his head, but Craig managed to demonstrate the ability with alarming clarity. "She's not even here and you're trying to kiss her boots."

Rolling up the map, Daniel shoved it ungratefully into his saddlebag. "It's better than I could do, is all," he lied, the weight of Craig's superiority over him making each word feel thick and bitter on his tongue. Every rustle of the trees seemed to carry his father's voice, his teachings: respect, obedience, enthusiasm to serve his betters.

Daniel shifted in his saddle for the umpteenth time and shuffled his thoughts like playing cards. If he re-dealt them enough times, maybe he'd figure out a way to reorganize his actions, lay out his hand in such a way that it wasn't so much of a blatant lie. Half-truths, he decided. Fibs instead of falsehoods.

"What do you want, soldier?"

The statement jarred Daniel from his mental recalibration. "Pardon?"

"What are you doing here?" Craig said with a grunt as he hacked away at some sapling branches set on impeding their way. "Why are you at this war front? I know it's not to lick boots and die. What has you so determined to appease the powers that be? Advancement?"

Daniel shook his head, surprised at the sudden line of questioning. "I don't have any interest in advancement." The mere thought set the muscles in his lower back to contracting. Advancement would mean more responsibility and more time at war. More time at war was less time spent with Willow, and a longer period waiting for his life to actually begin. "I want to serve the Empire Solaris and then —" Daniel sighed softly. "And then earn my payment for it so I can give my bride-to-be the life and home she both desires and deserves."

He didn't know what reaction he expected from baring his dreams, but it certainly wasn't laughter.

"Are you truly so incapable of talking openly?" Craig wheezed. "Just looking to collect some gold for your future bride? A humble Eastern farmer's dream, that."

"Well, I am a humble Eastern farmer." Craig's words were like tiny pin pricks across his skin. Respect was given blindly to those with titles, he mused sourly—given with the faith that those people may have gained their titles through honorable means, and would use the loyalty of their followers for good. All Craig had done was insult him at every turn. "And you would be best not to—"

Craig held up a hand, stopping Daniel short. It may as well have been a physical slap to the face.

"I will not be—"

"*Shh*," Craig hissed.

Daniel obliged with more reluctance than he would have wanted to admit, suddenly aware of the look on Craig's face.

"Do you hear that?" The lieutenant swiveled in his saddle, inspecting their surroundings.

Daniel gave everything a good look, but there wasn't much to behold. Greenery as far as the eye could see. The North had at least triple the trees as it did people.

"I don't hear anything," he said finally.

Craig settled back into his saddle, albeit somewhat uneasily. He had a look about him like someone had placed cool water on his seat. "Perhaps it was just the wind..." He trailed off, looking forward through squinted eyes. "Daniel, are you certain we're going the right way?"

"Of-of course I am." Another lie, a reflex this time; he wasn't and knew it.

"I would think we should've hit the burning from the last battle by now." Craig held out his hand. "Let me see the map."

Reluctantly, Daniel searched through his saddlebag for the requested item. He knew Craig was likely a better fit for navigation—surely he'd had some practice being a Lieutenant under Raylynn—but Daniel loathed the idea of admitting he'd been wrong. Furthermore, the second he passed over the map, he would give away his lie. At best, he would be reprimanded. And at worst… at worst, he might suffer some kind of demotion.

Daniel's fingers gripped the parchment so tightly it crumpled some at the folds of his hand. He studied the ink lines for a long moment, glancing at the compass for comparison. They had been keeping to his northeasterly heading just fine.

I can do this, he told himself.

"I'm confident we're going the right way," he announced. "The compass hasn't changed. We likely haven't seen the burn because we've overshot, just a little."

"If we've overshot, then we've not been going the right way." Craig made a reach for the map.

"We'll just cut east now." Daniel rolled up the map and returned it and the compass to his bag. His chest tightened some as he latched it closed.

"As we should have done from the beginning." The lieutenant didn't sound upset. If anything, he sounded amused. And amusement, Daniel had begun to realize, was far, far worse.

"We still saved time," Daniel insisted. If he forced the words off his tongue, perhaps they would become true.

"As long as we're heading east now." As expected, Craig was the first to move. He steered his horse, adjusting the direction just slightly to change their course for a more easterly direction.

Daniel watched the movement intently. Craig had been too far away to see the compass. Which meant that Craig had known their heading all along.

Heat weighed on his shoulders, slicking his shirt to his skin under his jerkin. Still, a small chill wormed its way up his spine. It was a sensation Daniel didn't like and didn't feel often: guilt.

"Lieutenant—" He had to say something. He had to find some way to convey the odd position he'd found himself in. He needed to explain that usually, he'd never dream of overstating his credentials or capabilities. That he'd been well-intended, at the very least, all along. That there was just something about Craig that had gotten under his skin, it would seem, to the point that he could make neither excuses nor apologies.

Daniel never got another word in.

A roar of shifting leaves and breaking branches broke to their left. Daniel turned toward the sound on pure instinct.

"Get down!" Craig shouted, in the same moment his body slammed into Daniel's.

The wind knocked from his lungs and the world tilted wildly. Daniel's ankle twisted awkwardly in the stirrup as Craig's momentum carried him out of the saddle.

They landed heavily on the ground, scabbards clattering like thunder. But the sound was dull compared to the scream from Daniel's horse. Over Craig's shoulder he looked up to see an arc of blood slicing through the open air, ribbons of red splattering overhead as if in slow motion. Daniel's eyes widened.

A giant feline pulled the horse to the ground by its neck. Teeth half the length of Daniel's sword and three times its width dug into the equestrian flesh, large claws making quick work of the last of the struggling horse's life. Spooked by the death of its companion, Craig's horse reared then fled the carnage at a gallop.

The attacking beast considered pursuit, its attention drawn momentarily to the bolting horse. But as Craig rolled to his feet, it turned its attention to the two prone men. Daniel had heard of the noru cat, the massive creatures Northerners trained to ride into battle. But they were rare, and he'd never seen one in person.

Though it would seem he was seeing one now.

The noru's rarity was no surprise; all one had to do was glance upon the beast to know why there weren't more roaming the wilds. Daniel could hardly breathe in the presence of the massive animal and wouldn't want it anywhere near a town he or a loved one was living. He couldn't fathom seeing such an animal and proceeding to try and wrangle and tame it enough to ride into battle, as the Northerners did.

In the golden sheen of the fearsome cat's eyes, Daniel could see the trembling silhouette of his own reflection.

I have already lost one prey, those eyes seemed to say. Daniel had no doubt that it was now even more resolved not to lose the rest of its meal. Daniel swallowed hard.

It seemed he was next on the menu.

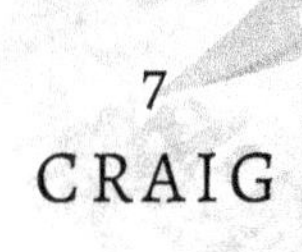

7

CRAIG

B Y THE MOTHER, it just *had* to be a noru cat.

They couldn't have simply spent a day wandering lost in the wilderness waiting for Daniel to admit that he'd led them astray. No, they had to end up horseless, facing down a beast with the speed and nimbleness of a field mouse, but the power and endurance of a thoroughbred Warstrider.

They were screwed.

Craig rolled off Daniel as the giant cat-like creature made quick work of the other man's horse. He shifted his feet, softened his knees—prepared to strike. His hands were at his hips, ready to spring upward. He had to make a break for it while the creature was distracted.

Just when Craig was about to move, the monster turned its attention toward them, its golden eyes flickering with hunger and bloodlust. Long crimson streaks dripped down its muzzle. Craig heard every drop spatter onto the forest floor with frightening clarity. It was as if the Mother had bestowed upon him an enhanced sense of hearing, the better to notice the sounds foretelling his imminent death.

"What do we do?" Daniel whispered. Craig couldn't help but flinch. He'd all but forgotten the man was there.

Why did I save him? The soldier had been nothing but a hassle this whole time, and his inadequacy had now landed them in a terrible mess. Daniel was stubborn and strong-willed and didn't know when to quit. Letting the noru feast on his obsequious tongue would have certainly prevented Raylynn from taking him under her wing...

"Craig?" Daniel's whisper was strained and tense, pressed through the corner of his mouth as though the cat's over-sized ears wouldn't be able to pick up the words. Craig tightened his grip on the hilt of his sword, fingers practically cramping beneath the strain.

If he had just left Daniel to die, he'd still have his horse. In those few precious moments, he could have been making a break for it. The noru would've been distracted chewing on the soldier Craig had little and less love for...

"*Craig?*"

"Here's what we do..." Craig spoke low and slow, not wanting to alert the beast prematurely. "I've heard their eyesight isn't as good as we think, that it's all in their hearing."

"Yeah, yeah, I've heard that too," Daniel agreed hastily.

"Good."

Daniel had most certainly *not* heard of that particular fact, because Craig had made it up on the spot.

"So I need you to lie down, get low, and stay still."

Daniel eased himself to the forest floor, wincing as his sword scabbard clanked. The noru cat watched intently, its ears swiveled forward and its eyes thinned to slits.

That's a good, giant man-eating beast, Craig praised mentally. *Focus on the tasty Eastern snack.*

Once Daniel was in place, his eyes flicked back up to Craig, though he seemed reluctant to look away from the noru for long. "Now what ?" His breathing was even louder than his forcefully restrained words.

"Now... you..." Craig shifted slightly between every few words. "You just lie there... And I..." He wound up his muscles, tensing his body like a coiled spring. He should've left Daniel to fend for himself from the beginning. It was never too late to correct one's mistakes. "I'll run."

Craig released the coiled energy in a half-leap to his feet.

"Wha—?!" Daniel couldn't get the words out. Even if he could, Craig would've barely heard him over the crunching of leaves, snapping of branches, and roar of the animal as he made his hasty escape. "You bastard!"

Craig glanced over his shoulder. Daniel was on his knees, unable to get further than that before the beast was upon him. In less than a breath, he brandished his joke of a sword —Craig was almost impressed at how quickly he had drawn it from its sheath.

The noru cat lunged and Daniel stabbed. The sword knocked against the animal's teeth, glancing just shy of the soft palette and missing its mark. It lodged itself through the cat's cheek, poking through the side of the animal's face with a small burst of blood. It was a fearless attack, one that Craig hoped would buy him more time to escape.

The animal hissed in pain, then let out a low, yowling keen. Craig forced his eyes forward again. Couldn't well leave a man behind and then lose his lead by craning his neck over his shoulder. A man as inept as Daniel was bound to have gotten killed somewhere along the way. War was far from kind to men like him; there wasn't much of a need for Craig to feel guilty over it.

Another roar sounded at his back. Craig half-turned, wanting to get a look at how close the animal was on his heels. What he'd expected to find was the cat bounding toward him. What he saw instead was the creature stunned at the scene of the attack, a bloody socket where his right eye should be. It shook its head in obvious pain and confusion, while Daniel sprinted toward Craig with alarming speed.

"Get back here and help—" Daniel vaulted over a low-hanging branch with a grunt. "—you coward!"

"Me?" Craig spun around a tree, deciding to dart farther into the forest on a diagonal tangent. It made no sense for them to run the same path; the cat would just kill them both. "I'm the coward?"

"Yes! You *are* the coward!" Daniel panted back, dipping around another branch. "Who leaves a fellow soldier to die?"

"Someone smart!" Craig didn't dare say more. A glance back at the cat revealed its single eye trained viciously on Daniel. If an animal could seethe vengeance, the noru would be wearing his intentions like a second coat of fur.

"You're intelligence is going to get us both killed!" While Daniel spoke, he leapt to grab the wide branch of a sapling. Twisting and pulling, he turned to face the wild beast. The noru cat was nearly upon him. Daniel gave a last mighty tug before releasing the small tree. Its green wood swung back into place, smacking the beast across the muzzle and dazing it once more.

Craig nearly tripped at the sight, unexpectedly impressed. Daniel might not be so useless after all. If he could muster half the thoughtfulness and skill he was demonstrating here in situations where he wasn't in mortal danger, the man might have some real value. Then again, the next moment saw Daniel making for a nearby tree, his intentions to climb it plain. Craig's stride faltered.

"Don't do that!" he yelled.

"What?" Daniel shouted back over the screech of the reeling cat.

"They can climb as well as they can sprint."

"How do I know I can trust you? You left me to die!" Daniel was two branches up in his foolish mission already.

"The actions of a man so focused on self-preservation that he would leave an idiot to die, even if that idiot is a fellow soldier, are actions worth trusting," Craig offered, but he was beyond wasting any more time on Daniel's mortality. If he wanted to get himself killed, Craig wouldn't stand in his way.

But it seemed Daniel would heed his advice after all. He leapt like a madman into the open air and landed in a tuck, rolling on the forest floor. He was lucky they were in the jungle; had they been back in the Southern tundras, the ground would've been hard as rock and far less forgiving.

Craig focused ahead of him. Branches scraped his face and body, snagging at his clothing and holding him back. Hot, visceral determination welled up from deep inside him; he would fight forest and noru and Northerner alike until he got what he wanted—that damned golden bracer. Nothing was going to stop him.

As he struggled against the forest, a twin of Raylynn's hastily scribbled map unfolded in his mind. He recounted every step and misstep that had led them to where they were now. The forest inspired its own sort of vertigo, but the land spoke to Craig. It always had.

He adjusted his course. For the first time in several

breaths, Craig glanced back over his shoulder. Daniel was red in the face and heaving—but he was still alive.

"I know how we can lose it!" Craig shouted.

"Why don't we just kill it?" The animal was gaining on them. Even with Daniel's clever use of the forest as defense, the noru could only be delayed so long.

"You think the two of us can bring it down?"

"We can't run forever." Daniel side-stepped some small trees that the cat bounded through without a problem.

"We won't."

They only had to find a hideaway large enough for both of them to fit into, but small enough that the noru cat couldn't get to them—a place strong enough to withstand the animal's inevitably frustrated attempts at entry. "Trust me, Daniel, and just do as I say."

"Trust you! *Trust you?*"

"Or don't, and see how you end up!" Either way, Craig was going for the one shot they had—the one and only place he could think of that might shelter them from the noru.

Their fates hung on his assumptions about their location. If he was wrong...

Well in that case, they were both as good as dead.

8

DANIEL

TRUST HIM.

TRUST him?

Of all people, Craig was the absolute *last* person Daniel was inclined to trust after what the lieutenant had done—which amounted not only to leaving him in peril, but orchestrating his death to aid in his own escape. Daniel cursed under his breath between gasps of air. No, Craig was no longer "lieutenant"; he lost that distinction the moment he acted so dishonorably. Daniel was prepared to let him know it, too.

If they actually survived this.

His sides burned, every breath stoking the fire that raged from his feet to his lungs. He couldn't keep pace for much longer. Soon, his legs were going to give out and he would be left at the mercy of the noru, the animal seemingly determined to consume him whole.

Daniel glanced over his shoulder, regretting it instantly. Every time he looked, the beast was that much closer, gaining ground on him with every guttural growl. It wouldn't be long before he looked and the animal's teeth would be a whisker's length away and primed to sink into his flesh. He needed to do something to delay the noru cat once more.

But what?

Daniel's eyes darted around, looking for anything that could be of help. Instinctively, he looked up. In the forest, death came from above. But, this time, it appeared that there their salvation also lay.

He hoisted himself onto one of the low tree branches, scaling as fast as he could. His legs protested every motion and his foot slipped as his fatigued muscles gave out for the first time. Daniel let out a grunt as he tried to cling onto the trunk of the tree.

"What are you doing?" Craig called from below and ahead. "I told you they could climb trees!"

"I know!" Daniel called back. There wasn't any time to explain. "I'm counting on it."

As if on cue, the noru cat leapt for the tree behind him. It sunk its long claws into the bark, peeling back layers until the razor-sharp talons gained purchase. Bending its powerful legs, it dug in its back claws and worked to find footing, aiming to get to where Daniel had scaled.

The branches were now as large around as his waist, and climbing was becoming difficult. Sweat soaked through his clothing and his leather felt like lead, weighing his shoulders down. He wasn't as high as he would've liked… but he *should* have enough space to clear the vines he'd seen from the forest floor below.

There wasn't even time to catch his breath. The noru cat had almost made it to him and Daniel looked between the animal and a shrub tree. The bit of foliage suddenly seemed half a world away, almost hidden behind a moss-laden veil of thick vines. Every instinct told him to jump, to run, but Daniel waited. He waited long enough for the noru cat to gain balance, to build strength and speed.

That's right, Daniel thought, *come and get me.*

The second he saw the animal's claws leave the bark, Daniel jumped. He angled himself, feet first, through one of the narrow openings that the interlocking sections of the vines created. The shrub tree he'd eyed below caught him with a thorny embrace. The jungle was determined to repay Daniel back for what he'd done to one of its own it would seem, a spindly branch nearly gouging out his right eye and making him a mirror of the noru cat he'd wounded minutes before.

Daniel tumbled, falling from branch to branch, his muscles not heeding to his commands to catch himself. With a thud, he landed onto the damp earth below, a pillow of leaves making for soft release. Daniel opened his eyes with apprehension at the roar that filled the air around him then, the sound reverberating into his very bones.

The beast had leapt after him and straight into the thick vines of the Northern jungle. The foliage was as dense as several ropes woven together, holding just as strong. The noru cat twisted and writhed, but the more it fought the more entangled it became.

"I can't believe that worked," Craig took the words right from dry and panting mouth.

Daniel scrambled to his feet, moving as quickly as he still could to catch up with the other man. "It won't hold for long."

"Obviously." They were now close enough that Craig no

longer had to shout to be heard. Though, he still half-shouted anyway.

Daniel stayed out of arm's reach to help resist the urge to punch the lieutenant across the face. "Where are we going?" he asked as they started running again, opting to save his arguments and possible fisticuffs for later.

"We're not far from The Pass." Craig didn't seem in much better shape than he. Blood and bruises mixed with sweat and dirt across all visible skin. "There're caves all around there. We can hide in the smallest one we find."

"*That's* your big plan? To find a hole to crawl into?"

"You have something better?" Craig snapped back. "Maybe use your keen sense of direction to get us out of this?"

A mighty thud drew attention to their backs and both men stalled. The noru cat had clawed or bitten its way out of the vines. Daniel watched as its darkly spotted fur rippled from the spasms of the muscles underneath it.

"Think the fall killed it?" he breathed.

"As if we'd be that lucky." Craig cursed loudly as the beast swayed and stood, shaking its massive head. Daniel's blows appeared to be taking their toll, however, the beast taking longer and longer to recover. But recovered, like death itself animated in the wilds of the Northern jungle. "Come on."

They started sprinting again, their lead only marginally more comfortable. Daniel wanted to ask how far, exactly, they were from these caves. But doing so would require him to use his mouth for something other than breathing or throwing up—and his body told him those were the only two options at present.

With a flash, a sunbeam permeated the canopy in the distance, illuminating a distinctly Southern piece of armor discarded on the ground. Daniel glanced at it in confusion—and the picture came into focus at once.

The trees in the distance had been bent back, char marks discoloring the ground. There had been a battle there. Which meant… He looked up and caught the corner of a building in the distance before it was hidden again.

"I think we're near the second Northern encampment we torched!" he cautioned, well remembering the fights they encountered in the strongly fortified outposts.

"Nonsense." Craig didn't mince words. "I know exactly where we are."

"If I navigated correctly, then—"

"Which you didn't!"

"You don't know that!"

"I do. You were just too proud to—" Craig ran wide around a tree and disappeared with a yelp.

"Craig!" Daniel scurried around to the other side of the tree, stopping just short of a gaping hole in the earth. His breath caught in his throat at the sight of the other soldier.

"Bloody Northern trap!" Craig's voice echoed from the rocky hole in the ground below. "Get me out of here!"

Craig's leg had been impaled on a sharp spear of wood embedded at the base of the pit. Lucky as he was that his leg—rather than his head—had been compromised, the injury eliminated any possibility of outrunning the most nimble predator in the jungle. Daniel looked around for a solution, racking his mind for some kind of way out—something, *anything*.

But there was nothing.

"I don't know what to do," he confessed.

"Don't you leave me, Daniel!" Panic crept into Craig's voice.

"Like you left me?" Anger boiled over and he returned to the ledge. "Maybe I *should* leave you there to fester and rot."

Craig's face was bright red and taut. "Then I hope the cat eats you alive."

The cat.

The snapping of brush and thundering of gigantic, heavy paws alerted Daniel to the situation at hand. He was all out of ideas, and he couldn't run any longer. He looked at the hole Craig had found himself in.

"Don't just stand there, do something!" Craig cried out. Annoyance and terror warred equally in his tone.

The only thing Daniel could think of was adapting their initial plan; he had to find somewhere to hide from the beast and wait out its interest.

With the last of his energy, Daniel pushed a broken branch, wood old and thick as his thigh, toward the hole. "Look out!" he shouted, offering no further warning. He couldn't be bothered for more than that. If he *accidentally* killed Craig now, he wouldn't exactly feel guilty.

Tipping the thick branch, Daniel let it fall into the crevice. He dove in after it just as the noru cat burst through the last of the saplings and lunged for him. Daniel felt the wind from the beast's jump whiz over his head as he half-slid, half-tumbled down the branch, clinging to it awkwardly to try to break his fall all while avoiding an untimely demise at the hands of the deadly spikes.

A fearsome yowl, part blood-lust and part frustration, echoed from above. From the lip of the pit, the noru lunged and snarled, batting helplessly into the mouth of the hole. But just as Daniel had suspected, the narrow opening was too small for the enormous cat to enter.

The beast managed to get itself in the hole from paw to

shoulder. It swung wildly, its paw a pendulum of swords, trying desperately to grasp them. Daniel pressed against the wall between two boulders and Craig lay back between the spikes, blood continuing to pool ominously around his impaled calf.

The noru reared back. Dirt and leaves fell around them like rain, shaken loose by the animal's frustrated trouncing above. It lunged once more. With a deafening snap, the branch Daniel had used to crawl into the cavern snapped, falling in two useless pieces, one narrowly missing Craig.

The beast repeated the process three more times before it seemed to tire. Daniel panted, continuing to watch the opening, listening for the growls and snarls of their deadly pursuer.

For the first time all afternoon, the forest was silent.

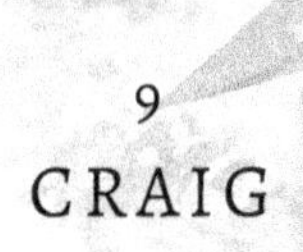

9

CRAIG

OUT OF THE frying pan, and into the fire.

Craig groaned in equal parts pain, frustration, and sheer disbelief at his luck. Every muscle in his body ached. His back screamed, shooting daggers of protest at his every attempt to move. Even craning his neck felt nearly impossible.

Not that he knew why he'd want to look closer at his situation. He could feel the sharp pain in his calf, so overwhelming that he was already going numb with shock. He was well aware of how he'd landed, and he knew the probability of him making it out of the jungle alive had plummeted to nearly zero.

Craig blinked up at the oculus of the cavern above him. He would've thought facing his own mortality would be harder. Then again, he'd had practice. How many times had he seen death on the battlefield? In the faces of those he'd killed? If death was coming for him, it would come with the familiarity of an old friend. It would come to collect the debt he'd exacted from so many.

As if summoned by his macabre, a face suddenly appeared before him, familiar and utterly unwanted. Craig blinked, wishing for the grim visage of the Father coming to take his immortal soul to the night realms beyond.

Instead he saw Daniel.

Craig tried to get a read on the man's expression, but the filtered sunlight above grew weaker by the minute, and it was getting harder to see.

"You're one lucky bastard," Daniel said finally.

"How do you figure?" Craig certainly didn't feel lucky, and he'd think the reasons why would be obvious. *Slow, imminent death* topped the list at the moment.

"You managed to outrun a noru cat in the jungle. You found somewhere to hide, *and* you didn't die in the process." Daniel listed off each one on his fingers, pointing finally at the wooden spikes on either side of Craig's head and chest. Both could've easily pierced one of his vital organs if he'd landed just slightly differently. "You got a lucky break on how this snapped, too." He nudged one of the large pieces of timber he'd used to get into the pit with his boot.

Craig was about to remark on Daniel's bad puns, but instinct told him to let the silence linger. There was something to it. Something he hadn't felt around Daniel yet. Something that could only be described as kinship between two soldiers—true warriors. Narrowly escaping death together would do that, he supposed. All sorts of rushes going through his mind and body right now. Perhaps the adrenaline was turning him mad.

In less than a beat, their accord grew heavier. "And you're also pretty damn lucky I didn't leave you to die after what you did." Daniel stared down at him, a challenge settling across his brow.

But Craig had no intention of denying it. He wasn't entirely sure what he'd have done in Daniel's shoes, in fact. So Craig said simply, "At least I can say now that you're not completely useless. Every soldier goes through some hazing." His indifferent tone was greatly marred by the slight wheezes of pain he couldn't quell, making the overall effect almost sardonic. Teasing.

As such, Daniel snorted, squatting down next to Craig's leg. Without warning, he began hacking into the spear currently sawing through Craig's calf. Craig would have wondered how the other man had managed to hold onto his stupid fancy sword during their flight through the jungle, but all humor vanished as each reverberation exploded stars behind his eyes. Daniel continued to work, obscured behind the blur of Craig's pain.

Craig let out an animalistic noise that rivaled the noru's earlier yowling, as Daniel placed both hands on either side of his leg and lifted. His appendage came free of the spear with a sickening, slick sort of popping sound. Darkness framed the edges of his vision. He'd known pain in battle before, been cut up something fierce, in fact, but this level of agony was new, even for him.

It was like a fire burned up his leg in searing waves that terminated in his head. The edges of his consciousness singed, darkening everything to black.

He blinked, trying to clear his vision, and slowly, thankfully, sensations came back to him. The pain was first. No longer a sharp or unbearable stabbing, it was now more of a dull ache that lingered like a phantom presence in every breath.

Craig blinked again. This time, when his eyes opened, he cursed the light that failed to come back to him. Everything was dark. Glowing shapes flickered in and out against the blackness.

"You awake?" a familiar voice asked from across the narrow space.

Narrow space.

That was right. They had been chased by a noru cat. They'd landed in a pit… Craig turned his head toward the voice.

The spikes that had been sunk into the rocky earth had all been uprooted and were now burning in a crude fire pit. Daniel sat diagonally from him, looking worse for wear, one sleeve mostly missing.

Craig looked down to his leg and quickly solved the mystery of the missing sleeve. Wound tightly around his calf was a makeshift bandage. What wasn't bloodstained was the same color as the shirt Daniel wore under his jerkin.

"You passed out when I was freeing you from that spike."

"You could have warned me first," Craig muttered, recalling the sudden, mind-numbing effect of Daniel's earlier ministrations. He wanted to be angrier, but it was difficult to muster the emotion.

"I could have," Daniel agreed, leaning back onto the rocky wall behind him. "But that would have defeated the purpose of the hazing. Isn't that what soldiers do?"

Craig rolled his eyes.

Daniel rolled his own in a perfect imitation.

Craig began to chuckle, a soft, bubbling laughter that only seemed capable of growing, consuming him from chest to throat and out into the suffocating air of the pit.

"Have you gone mad, now?" Daniel passed his fire poker from hand to hand. Craig only continued to laugh.

"Looks like you're not completely useless."

"Madness it is." Daniel sighed, exhaling a bit of profanity.

"Now, this is what I've wanted all along." Craig shifted with a wince, trying to get a better seated position.

"What?"

"You to speak to me frankly. To see who you really are underneath the facade of the perfect common soldier," he clarified.

Daniel snorted obnoxiously. "You saw who I really was. You didn't like it. Now you've got this."

"I like this better."

It was Daniel's turn to chuckle. "Are all lieutenants like you?"

"Only the worthwhile ones." Craig thought of Raylynn and her unique charisma, her arrogance, her easy, confident nature. It was vastly different from Jax's wild madness, that tugged apart his sanity from moment to moment. Still, the two shared certain similarities. Craig had been trying to embody their mannerisms from the first moment Raylynn had taken him under her wing.

Raylynn. His whole life had begun to revolve around her for the sake of a golden bracer. Perhaps that was why he had been so hard on Daniel from the get-go: part of him feared the notion that Raylynn might use the other man as a sort of replacement.

"How did you start the fire?" Craig asked, genuinely curious. A peace offering.

"We're trained to carry an emergency kit, strapped around the waist, just in case. Mine always contains a flint." Daniel held up a flat sort of satchel that Craig had only seen once in training. After that brief exposure to the kit, him and everyone he knew promptly forgot of its existence; it was restricting and cumbersome, so they saw little point. In fact, the only thing he'd thought to strap to his person in months was the letter for Baldair. A small motion affirmed the missive was still attached around his waist.

An emergency kit. Craig couldn't stop his laughter. It reverberated off every wall of the pit like beats on a drum, no doubt echoing up into the forest above. *Oh well*, he thought. If their luck continued as it had so far, there would be Northern soldiers on them at any second.

But none came, and Craig considered it to be the first good grace of the Mother they'd had since their journey began.

"You *would* carry that with you," Craig hummed, amused.

"And you should be glad I did." Craig almost—*almost*—felt guilty for his continued teasing. Almost but not quite. "Because now we have fire to keep us warm and you have healing salve—not enough, but some."

It took a long, pregnant pause, but eventually, Craig caved. "I am glad," he confessed softly.

"What was that?"

Craig knew Daniel had heard him, but he obliged him anyway. Reluctant as he was to admit it, the soldier had earned his praise and gratitude. "I'm relieved for your quick thinking, both in your foresight to bring that with you, and earlier with the noru." The pause that followed seemed practically companionable.

"Careful—that sounds like appreciation," Daniel said skeptically.

"Because it was." Craig smirked, yawning. Even moving his head to do that little hurt. His whole body continued to ache, though Daniel's salve explained why he was no longer in terrible pain.

Craig cast a weary eye on the other man, looking for any

grave wounds he might have endured. Seeing nothing, Craig tilted his head back.

"I don't know how we'll get out of here," Daniel admitted softly.

"I don't either." Craig shrugged. "But you seem to be pretty clever, actually."

"Don't act so surprised."

Craig huffed in amusement. "Not every day you meet a clever Eastern farmer."

"Then you haven't met enough Eastern farmers."

"Fair enough." Craig yawned again, and again a shooting pain seared down his jaw. "You can tell me all about your clever friends in the morning. I'm sure you'll think of something then, too."

Craig didn't hear if Daniel replied. Too quickly, and without his consent, his body gave into exhaustion.

10

DANIEL

W HEN DAWN CAME, his eyes had crusted almost completely shut.

Daniel rubbed his face with the pads of his hands, smearing dirt and grime across aching muscles and stinging cuts. Blearily, he forced his eyes open, trying to pull his mind together. His body hurt, but it was still in one piece. No Northerners or noru cats had gotten into their hiding place in the night; he and the lieutenant had both somehow lived to see another dawn.

He tilted his head at the thought, letting his eyes drift over to the other man currently occupying their cramped space. Craig hadn't moved since he'd passed out the night before, but the steady rise and fall in his chest was reassuring. Daniel breathed a sigh of relief. One really did have to find joy in the small things in life.

His eyes followed the still-curling smoke from the remnants of last night's fire, tendrils of grey floating in wisps up through their only portal to the world beyond. The cavern was shaped like a jug, its thin neck above the only way out. Daniel sat straighter, taking stock of his surroundings. If Craig was going to survive, he'd need more medicine. If they were *both* going to survive, they'd need other essentials as well.

Daniel shifted his feet and his knees popped in protest. His muscles were angry with him, his joints brutalized, but his body didn't betray him. Even after the abuse they'd taken, his limbs heeded his commands.

Craig came to life with a groan. The lieutenant came around slowly, his body waking before his mind. Daniel couldn't stop him as he tried to move his leg on instinct, hissing immediately.

"Sorry. It wasn't all a bad dream, I'm afraid."

"An—" Craig's voice cracked. He licked his lips and blinked to clear his vision. "And here I expected to wake up to hoards of young lasses throwing themselves at me." His attempt at humor was strained at best, but oddly appreciated.

"I hear that happens upon our glorious return." Daniel began shuffling around the perimeter of the cavern, feeling along the stone.

"It'll be your first time returning from the front, right? This is your first tour?"

Daniel nodded before realizing Craig couldn't actually see him from where he sat. "It is."

"Aren't you just having a grand time?"

"I didn't enlist to have a grand time." None of the stones had any sort of budge or wiggle so far.

"Then why did you enlist?"

Daniel walked back around to where Craig could see him, already exhausted. He leaned against a stone for support. "As I told you—I simply want to make a life for myself and my betrothed. I'll serve my country and take what's owed me, no lasses or fanfare required."

"Ah yes. That's right. Spoken like a man who has someone waiting for him." Craig gave a smile and for the first time, it seemed genuine. "Your betrothed. Tell me of her."

"Her name is Willow." Just saying it aloud gave him strength. The beautiful hazel eyes of his bride-to-be glowed in his mind's eye. "And if I don't get us out of here, I'll never see her again." That would be a fate worse than death, as far as Daniel was concerned.

"Well, surely you may be able to climb it?"

"No. I thought about it, but the ceiling is too sheer and perpendicular to the walls... There's no way I could make a jump for the opening either." Daniel didn't give the thought any more consideration. He had other things to focus on.

"What are you looking for?"

"Another way out."

"Why do you think there is one? Whoever dug the trap was likely raised out by a rope."

Daniel stopped, frustrated more with his own fruitless line of logic than with Craig's interrogation of it. "This cavern wasn't dug by hand. There are no tool marks anywhere, and the walls are too sheer to have been manually crafted."

"A Groundbreaker, then."

"I thought about that." Daniel had always found sorcery fascinating, though he'd rarely encountered it before his time in the army. Even then, most sorcerer-soldiers spent their time focused on the Black Legion, rarely mingling with their brothers beyond the group. "But it seems too... flawed.

If this was made with magic alone, I would've expected it to be more perfect."

"Like the walls surrounding Soricium." The flawless, impenetrable barrier that surrounded the capital of the North famously insulated the beating heart of the last bastion standing against the Empire Solaris.

"Exactly." Daniel returned to exploring the cavern. "So, my thought is that this was a natural cavern they expanded on… You said we were near the pass and that such things were more common, right?"

"I did." Uncertainty laced Craig's words. The man clearly had some doubts after falling into the remnants of a Northern outpost's trappings.

"Then, I'm sure—"

The boulder Daniel pushed against budged, just slightly, as he put his weight against it. He pushed a little harder, and harder still. On the third shove he was met with a small sigh of air, like the quiet exhale of a secret.

"I'm sure there's another way out," Daniel announced triumphantly.

At Daniel's tone, Craig willed himself to brave his body's protests and turn to gather a look of his own.

Daniel peered into the sliver of darkness he'd exposed. He could see nothing, which meant he had to open the portal further. He put his shoulder against the boulder. His legs slid and scraped against the stone, sending loose gravel skittering across the cavern floor. With every movement, his legs threatened to give way, to send him sliding face first into the boulder. Still, he pushed.

It was time for their luck to shape up, if only for just a while, and this certainty kept Daniel at his task even after his body begged for mercy. A line of sweat had begun to trace down his spine by the time Daniel shifted the boulder enough to shimmy through. He couldn't see much further down the supposed path, but he could see enough to know it wasn't a dead end.

"Well?" Craig demanded finally.

"It looks promising." Daniel glanced at the sky above. There was still plenty of daylight if—*when*—he found a way out. Still, just in case…

Daniel broke off large spears of wood from the branch he'd used the day prior to descend into the pit. He collected up the scraps and scooped up sawdust from where it'd splintered, bringing it all to the ashen remnants of the fire from the night before.

"The tunnel is dark, so I'm going to need some fire, for light," he explained as he collected the flint from his emergency satchel. Daniel hated using his sword as a striker, but he didn't have any other steel on hand. "Plus, in case I'm gone after dark… you'll have a fire."

It took him four tries to get a spark off the stone, the wood shavings finally catching with a wisp of smoke. Daniel quickly flipped flat onto his stomach and began to blow gently on the glowing bits of wood. Fire quickly consumed them, burning upward against the other smaller bits. It was fleeting and bright, but hot enough to catch the other kindling that would then build a proper fire.

"Here." Craig ripped off one of the scraps that still clung to his trousers, remnants hanging in loose tatters where Daniel had cut back to bandage his wound. "Wrap this around your fire stick. Wish I had some tar or oil to coat it in."

Daniel accepted the kindness and did as Craig suggested. "This will do well enough… It'll burn for a little, catch the wood… Then I can always snuff it and use the embers."

"Navigating by ember glow," Craig sniffed, smirk pulled a bit too tight. "Let's hope it doesn't come to that."

"Knowing our luck…"

Craig actually laughed at the remark. Their situation was odd, and borderline hopeless. When everything falls apart, what else is there but laughter?

"Good luck, Daniel," Craig said suddenly, just before Daniel disappeared into the tunnel. After everything they'd been through, Daniel found the genuineness in Craig's voice both surprising and expected.

"Thanks. I'll be back before you know it," Daniel said boldly, starting for the dark line against the stone wall. How he hoped those words would be true… How he'd do his best to make them so.

Twisting to the side, Daniel held the makeshift torch before him, the fire already reduced to a smolder. The walls of the tunnel lit up, narrow as it was, and continued on farther than Daniel could see. It was as good an option as any, especially considering it seemed to be the only option available to them. He gathered his bravery, ignored the pain in his fatigued muscles, and pushed onward.

11

CRAIG

DANIEL HAD BEEN gone for hours.

The man whom, a day ago, Craig had barely been able to tolerate, was now his only ally in what was quickly becoming a grim world to face. Especially alone. He felt like a lame horse waiting to be put out to pasture, or shot behind the barn. At least while Daniel was there, things seemed marginally less hopeless.

Other than consider his own thoughts, he had nothing to do to pass the time. Trouble was, Craig had always supposed his thoughts were the most boring thing about him. He'd never been particularly bright—as his father would remind him frequently—and he'd never managed to make it out of his hometown of Rivend, save for the month he'd enlisted as a soldier and, from there, marched North. All he had to think on were years of the same routine, day after day, in that sleepy little town. As much as it pained him to admit it, his pre-army life was remarkably similar to Daniel's.

The best thing about him, about his life, was going to be

joining the Golden Guard. A group, a family, friends, a purpose. He'd gain it all with just a strip of gold on his forearm.

Day faded to night, and Craig began to doze off from a mixture of pure exhaustion and boredom. An untold time later, he was jolted awake by a soft grunt and the scrape of boots against stone.

"Daniel?" He'd had all day, but he didn't think once to position himself so he could face the opening. Even if he had… what could he have done? Either it was Daniel, finally returning with news, or it was some Northerner coming to finish the job the trap had started. And if that were the case, facing the entryway would do little to stop it.

Craig's palms went slick. He would die without ever making lieutenant. He took a deep breath, trying to sturdy himself against the idea of a pointless death.

"It's me."

Craig couldn't begin to express the relief that coursed through him at hearing those two words. Still, he heard himself say "Took you long enough."

His wasn't actually annoyed by Daniel's return. Far from it. But the Easterner was the only receptacle for the anger he felt at himself. He was a soldier who sought a golden bracer; he should be above the fear of dying.

"I come bearing gifts." Daniel came around to Craig's line of sight and held out a sloth, neatly slaughtered and ready for cleaning.

"You went hunting? You can hunt?" Craig's mouth was already watering at the prospect of a meal.

"Well, I do have to eat. As do you." Daniel shrugged, dropping the carcass to the ground on the opposite side of the fire pit. Craig watched as he broke off more wood, using one particularly long and narrow stick as his new poker. With impressive and quick skill, he nurtured the fire back to life.

"I suppose the hunting is usually relegated to the soldiers…" Craig had never given it much thought. He'd spent more time learning under Raylynn than he had as an actual infantryman. He'd risen quickly though the ranks and in so doing, left certain necessities allotted to those beneath him.

"As it is now." Daniel spoke without looking up from skinning the animal. It was a clumsy hack job, with sharp rocks and his sword the only available tools for butchering, but it was better than Craig would've expected. In fact, it was better than he could've done under the circumstances. It betrayed a level of skill and familiarity for the task that even Craig had to admire.

"Springroot." Craig nodded at the handful of leaves Daniel had piled next to his makeshift workstation.

Daniel paused. "You know it?"

"I've been here longer than you have." Craig chuckled. Just when he was getting familiar with the man, Daniel reminded him that he was, indeed, green as ever. "Pass them here. I can tend to my wound while you do that."

"Would you like me to?" Daniel offered, still obliging Craig's wishes.

"I'm not some invalid." Craig took the plants from Daniel, relieved that the man didn't put up a fight on the matter. Certainly, it was easier to have someone tend to him than do it himself, but he didn't have that luxury right now. "I've done it before."

"Have you?"

Craig shot the other man an incredulous look. Daniel shrugged.

"You just seem very accustomed to the lifestyle of the higher officers." He couldn't seem to hide his smug smile, despite the way his eyes stayed focused on the sloth.

"You… You're calling me spoiled, aren't you?"

"Well?"

"Well what?" Craig couldn't believe that Daniel of all people would make such a bold implication.

"Aren't you?"

Craig burst out laughing.

Within his mirth he hid the hisses and grimaces he elicited while removing the makeshift bandage around his calf. It was a nasty wound, and unwrapping tugged at the ragged flesh with stomach-turning sharpness. Once he got a good look at it, though, he realized it wasn't nearly half as bad as what it could've been. It was free of splinters, and the tissue was angry but mostly clean.

"Here, use a bit to wash it first." Daniel was back at his side, holding out a hollow bit of wood. Inside sloshed water.

"Food, medicine, *and* water? Perhaps I'm spoiled after all." Craig took the vessel carefully.

"Perhaps." Daniel grinned as he took the water back, then disappeared behind Craig to store it safely out of reach.

His absence gave Craig enough time to compose himself in the wake of such a bold remark.

"All right, Daniel Taffl." He'd seen and heard enough. "What's your story?"

"My story?" Barely glancing in Craig's direction, Daniel began to shear meat from bone.

"You're supposedly some farmer from the East… But you

have a fancy sword on your hip and enough skill in using it to attract the attention of Raylynn Westwind. You're resourceful, clever—smart, even."

"Why do you sound so surprised at that last bit?" Daniel arched his eyebrows.

"Eastern farmers aren't really known for their... educations."

"And when did you last spend time in the East, lieutenant?"

It was either a lucky jab, or Daniel was even more astute than Craig gave him credit for. Though perhaps his lack of worldliness was simply that obvious. "Touché."

"My story isn't much," Daniel began after a moment. "I was born in the East, on a farm just outside of Paca. I played with pretend swords growing up using river reeds. That's why the thinner blades suit me better."

"More swishing and stabbing." It made sense enough. But that still meant Daniel had a decent bit of natural talent in his farmer's blood.

"I met a girl in town." Daniel segued without preamble.

"Willow."

"Yes, Willow." Daniel nodded. "She was the purveyor's daughter. A good woman, far better than a man like me deserves..."

"So you enlisted to give her a better future." Craig had heard the story dozens of times, twice yet from Daniel alone. There was really only one thing that drove a man or woman to do something as extreme as fight in a war: love. Be it for the love of another, the memory of a love lost, love of country (rare but possible, he supposed), or more often than not, the most practical kind of love—love of gold.

"She wants to move to the capital," Daniel went on,

oblivious to Craig's musings. "But I have no marketable skills in the city."

"Ah, so you hope to use this as an opportunity to fund a wedding, a new start, and earn a job in the palace guard?" Many soldiers, especially those of merit, were offered positions in the palace guard following the end of their enlistment period.

"Just so." Daniel skewered a piece of meat and held it over the tops of the flames. Craig already knew it was going to turn into a tough and tasteless hunk of char, but his mouth watered anyway. It had been days since he'd last had anything hot, and after the energy expended the day before, he'd take almost any edible sustenance. "What about you?" Daniel asked suddenly, and the question caught him off guard.

"Me?" Craig thought about his answer for a long moment, though he couldn't quite explain what made him hesitate. His story was no more special than Daniel's. He took a wad of leaves and stuffed them into his mouth, chewing them to a paste. The movement muddled the sap within, spreading a tingling feeling across his tongue and lips, and gave him time to think.

Without any concern for decorum, he spit out the paste into his hand and began to smear and press it into his wound. It should have some form of stitching, he noted, but that was well beyond their capabilities. Still, if he could keep it clean and medicated with springroot, it would heal quickly.

"Is there anyone else here?" Daniel asked when the silence had stretched on, reminding Craig that he hadn't answered.

"Well, you could've finally gone mad."

"With you to drive me there? Entirely possible."

Craig was set to laughing again. "This personality, Daniel. I rather like it. Don't turn back into the model soldier, alright?"

"I'm not sure I could even if I wanted to, now." Daniel put a second fillet on a new stick. Silence persisted, but Daniel's question still hung heavy in the air.

"My story, huh?" Craig thought aloud, deciding to give the man a real answer. "I'm afraid it's not as noble as yours."

"Mine's not that noble."

"Seeking out a better life for a woman you love? Sacrificing yourself for that future? Sounds fairly noble."

Daniel said nothing. He pulled the first stick from the fire and set the steaming meat aside to cool.

"Me? I'm just some kid from a small town called Rivend, a slice of nothing in the middle of Southern nowhere." He shrugged. "My friend Jon and I got it in our heads that it'd be a good idea to join the army, get out and see the world. I got a taste of what it would be like to be someone…" Craig thought of the first time Raylynn took an interest in him. Feelings of hope and possibility had blossomed in a patch of his soul he had otherwise thought barren. "Now that I know what that feels like, I don't want to give it up. And I'd do anything to defend it."

Daniel considered him for a long moment, his face utterly unreadable. Leaning forward, he plucked the stick from the dirt and held out the pointed end with the meat to Craig, who took it with a muttered word of thanks.

"I don't hear anything that isn't noble there." Daniel took the second stick from the fire, setting it aside for himself.

"You're following your own mission, your own dream… and that dream is in service to the Empire. It's far nobler than simply doing this for the ladies that supposedly throw themselves on you and fawn over your battle scars when you return."

"*Mmm*," Craig hummed, chewing. He shook his head with a forced swallow, reminding himself to eat slower. It'd be supremely embarrassing if he died choking to death after everything. "I'll gladly take the lasses, too."

They both laughed.

"So, your being Raylynn's lieutenant then… Is that fulfilling your dream?"

He could've simply said yes. It wouldn't have even been a lie. Becoming Raylynn's student, having the opportunity to excel, was far more than a nobody like him could hope to achieve. But it wasn't quite the fulfillment of his dream. No, that was yet to come.

"Almost," Craig confessed.

"Almost?"

"I want to become a member of the Golden Guard." Had Craig spoken his desire to anyone else, he would have expected it to be met with unbridled laughter. The Golden Guard, the most elite fighting force in the world, hand-picked by Prince Baldair himself… It wasn't a group anyone could just join at will.

But this strange Eastern farmer-turned-soldier didn't laugh—and Craig had known he wouldn't. Daniel chewed his hunk of meat thoughtfully before placing another round onto the fire.

"Well, then," Daniel mused aloud, "we shall see you with that bracer."

As though deeming the matter settled, Daniel turned

back to the carcass and continued to scrape the meat from its bones. Which left Craig to sit in stunned silence, looking over the man who had somehow managed to sneak his way up from rival to annoyance to amusement, and then more shockingly, from savior to friend.

12

DANIEL

TWO DAYS CAME and went with relative ease. *Relative* being the operative word. Daniel wouldn't exactly call it "comfortable" in the cavern they had made their temporary home, but it was as safe and protected as they could hope to be in hostile territory.

Even if they wanted or needed to move, however, their ability to do so would be severely limited by Craig's limp. The lieutenant was determined to continue his mission as soon as possible, a determination Daniel could respect. But his attempts at standing weren't doing either of them any favors.

"It will be a good test." Craig had somehow gotten it in his head that he would join Daniel on the morning's hunting and gathering trip.

"You don't need to test anything." Daniel itched at the side of his jerkin. He'd made a rudimentary attempt at getting clean in the nearby stream he'd been using as their water source, but it wasn't enough water for a proper bath. Beyond that, the idea of stripping down with the possibility of an enemy stumbling on him made Daniel nervous. A certain level of grime had settled in the cave as a kind of third companion.

"Prince Baldair will be wanting this letter. I have to—"

"I know you want to impress the prince." Daniel understood what it was to be on a mission, and felt Craig's dedication had cast the lieutenant in a new and favorable light. "But you're not impressing anyone if you die in the process from infection or an enemy attack."

"This area has been vacant of Northern activity for weeks." Craig pointedly ignored the idea of an infection, Daniel noticed.

"It's not impossible." Daniel adjusted his sword belt at the thought. "Besides, the more you rest, the faster and cleaner your wound will heal. If you push it, chances are you could have lasting damage in the leg. Think of how that would affect your swordsmanship."

Craig was silent. Daniel didn't need to spell it out further. It was said that Prince Baldair only solicited the most talented soldiers for his guard, those whose swordsmanship matched or exceeded his own considerable skill.

"I think I'll only need another day, thanks to the springroot."

"We'll see," Daniel agreed mildly. The springroot did wonders: numbed pain, promoted healing, and kept wounds covered in thick slime that kept out dirt and infection. But it wasn't a miracle cure. A proper cleric could've had Craig at full speed by now.

"I would like to request something other than sloth today, soldier." Craig put on an air of superiority.

"I shall do my best, lieutenant." Daniel played along, giving Craig a salute.

"See that you do, for when I have my golden bracer I will not forget what you've done for me here."

"You are too kind," Daniel said as he rounded the wounded man and squeezed himself into the narrow passage that led to the world beyond their sanctuary.

Daniel knew the tunnel by heart at this point. It was a simple walk and he'd made it a point to clear it of debris and rock as much as he could. Now he shimmied along the wall in the darkness, feeling the already familiar stone as it gnarled and curved round toward a spot of ambient light.

It was almost easy to forget that they were still at war. He had been focused for years on what was next: taking care of the farm, courting Willow, doing his best to secure a good life for her. He hadn't taken time on his own for as long as he could remember. Even in his present circumstances, he was learning there was something to be said for taking time for one's self. While this excursion paled in comparison to the hunting parties he'd heard men and women reminisce over with fondness around camp fires, and it was certainly not what he would've planned, it was surprisingly nice.

Minus the constant threat of death lurking behind every corner.

Daniel poked his head out of the opening to the narrow tunnel. Emerald shone brightly in every corner of his sight, contrasting the dim, gray cave that had been his home. Daniel gave his eyes a moment to adjust, taking in the sights and sounds, waiting tentatively for any potential threat to reveal itself.

But just as it had been the past two days, the world was calm and still. A stray breeze rustled the treetops. Dew drops turned wide, flat leaves into little drums, thrumming their own quiet song. Unseen animals rustled here and there as the jungle teemed with benign life.

The North was quite a beautiful place, actually, and vastly unlike anything else Daniel had ever seen. On the southern border of his home, the fringes of the great pine forests of the South began to spring from the hilly ground. He had thought them mighty the first time he'd laid eyes on them, headed to the capital with Willow. But now that he had seen the trees in Shaldan, nothing could ever compare.

Daniel trekked down what was now a familiar path toward the small stream. Brush thickened the nearer he got to the water, and he had to slowly make his way through. It would have been easier if he hacked it away, but Daniel didn't want to disturb the foliage more than necessary. It was best to leave as little trace of his existence as possible.

What Craig had said was true. The Imperial army had made a piercing attack to Soricium, the capital of the North, and then laid siege to the claimed land. After securing their foothold, the Emperor worked slowly outward, chipping away at the strength of the only remaining country on the Main Continent not under his control.

It was unlikely he'd encounter hostile forces this close to Soricium, especially in the wake of Raylynn's company. Their job had been to clear resistance seeking to flank the army. Water was one of those weird things in nature, however; a great equalizer, it brought together both predator and prey.

When Daniel heard the lifting tones of the Northern tongue, he wasn't sure which he was going to be.

He crouched low and pressed himself into the hollow of a nearby tree trunk. The voices were faint, barely audible over the sounds of the forest around him. But they were distinct. They were filled with words he'd heard shouted in hate at him countless times—as if he were the one who decreed the order to burn their homes and kill their friends. It could all be over if their head clan merely surrendered to the Empire.

Stay or retreat? If he stayed, he risked not only his life, but Craig's as well. Instinct told him to collect whatever information he might extract from his hidden vantage point. His training told him to investigate on behalf of the Empire, no matter the cost.

Instinct and training won out, as usual.

Slowly, cautiously, Daniel slunk forward. He made every attempt to be as inconspicuous as possible, pressing into each nook and cranny he could see as he neared the source of the noise. Through the thick foliage, he could make out the vague shapes of two figures, hunched together by the river.

They spoke purposefully. Their gestures and manner betrayed no desire to be subversive; clearly they thought themselves alone.

Daniel kept one hand on his sword hilt at all times. It kept the blade flush against him, at the ready, and prevented any sort of clanking from his scabbard.

The two Northerners continued to gesture between them, their tabards swaying with their movements. Daniel wondered what had them so entranced, and desperately wished he could understand some of the lyrical-sounding phrases being passed between them.

Slowly, he crept forward. Close enough to see the shades cast by their boots and the threading on their clothes. Close enough that they could hear when his foot slipped on a root and crashed through the underbrush.

The next thirty seconds seemed to drag in slow-motion.

Daniel's foot fell, hard, onto the fresh leaves and twigs he'd been trying to avoid. His ankle pulled awkwardly, just painfully enough to draw the hiss of a grimace across his mouth. The two Northerners turned instantly, looking directly at him.

The woman on the right with long braided hair raised their hand, and the trees seemed to shudder to life, scurrying and parting like bugs faced with a sunbeam. The branches and trunks arced outward and away from her focused gaze. Her eyes, the same color as the leaves she commanded, stared straight at him.

A sorcerer.

Wonderful.

Daniel gave into his training. He'd lost the element of surprise but that didn't mean he also had to lose the first strike as well. The moment his foot was stable under him again, Daniel pushed upward on the strength of his good leg.

The pommel of his sword was already warm from his grip on it. The blade was drawn with a bright *shiiing*, and not a moment too late. The woman twisted her hand and several branches jutted forward like spears waiting to impale him. The sword shone brightly, hitting off the spotted light, as Daniel arced it through the air, beating away the branches and sheering off their pointed tips.

The Northern man was flat-footed and clumsy, scrambling for the blade at his hip. If he wasn't attacking with magic as well, there was a chance Daniel was only dealing with one sorcerer. At the end of his sword swing, he brought his elbow to his waist, tucking it tightly. If he was right, the sorcerer should be dispatched first; magic was much harder to manage than blades.

Twisting his wrist slightly to put the point of his blade at the woman's face, Daniel did a quick double-step, readjusting his footwork and shifting his momentum to go into a second lunge. He had killed too many now to feel any hesitation for the act. His sword was straight and true, all the force he could muster behind it.

The woman twisted at the last second, bringing up her hand. His sword vibrated with a loud echo as it hit her palm. *Groundbreaker*, Daniel thought with searing frustration. Their magic enabled them to turn their skin as hard as stone, completely impenetrable by blades. There was only one spot that wasn't hardened…

Daniel slid a foot forward to bring his blade upward and around the woman's wrist, pointing right for her eye. She swung her free hand up, forcing Daniel to give up his attack to jump away and avoid a spear of roots summoned from deep within the earth at his feet. By now, the man had found his weapon and charged forward with a snarl of a word that Daniel didn't recognize but nonetheless assumed wasn't good.

The Northerner charged with a standard short blade, one that Daniel knew would beat him in power if he let it turn into that sort of battle. So Daniel focused on finesse. He disengaged, over-parrying the man's strike. The point of his blade drew a line up the Northerner's sword hand, shearing through tendons and drawing a cry of both pain and frustration from his enemy's lips as the man's hand was no longer capable of holding the sword.

Rather than going in for the kill, Daniel made a strategic retreat, taking the opportunity to re-engage the sorcerer. In almost every battle he'd endured, he'd been outnumbered. Why should now be any different? Victory wasn't about quick kills or grand attacks, but chipping away at an enemy's strength, doing what needed to be done.

Daniel was a cautious fighter in that regard. Just like his sword, he wasn't suited for charging in mindlessly and relying on brute strength. He found victory in the smallest of openings. His opponent need make only one tiny error, and the fight was as good as won.

Like when the man swung too wide, clumsy with only one hand on his sword.

Daniel slid back and angled his body so that when he pressed forward, he and the Northerner were shoulder to shoulder, facing different directions. The blade plunged into the man's throat, spurting blood from the jugular like a tap, and extending clean out the other side. His dying breath gurgled and his knees went loose. Daniel quickly withdrew his weapon before the collapsing deadweight could take it down with him.

When he turned, blade at the ready, the sorcerer was gone.

A rustling of leaves and swaying of branches brought his attention upward. High above, the woman stood. A vine snaked around one of her legs through to her middle and then across her arm, where she held onto it with tension.

They stared at each other. Two fighters from different sides of the field. Neither was operating under express commands to kill the other, merely the understanding that this was what being "enemies" meant. The woman squinted down at him before turning and stepping from the wide branch where she'd stood.

The vine pulled her upward magically. She rose into the canopy and disappeared into the leaves above. Daniel watched until the thick leaves stopped rustling and the forest was still—or, as still as it ever was—once more.

Daniel wiped the blood off his blade onto the dead man's tabard, and considered his next steps. The woman was no doubt making a tactical retreat… They were both random soldiers, and what point would it serve to attack each other as they were? Would she alert her allies to the rogue Imperial soldier she'd found? Or would she let the matter rest, a one-off skirmish that war produced by chance?

Daniel's thoughts were interrupted when his roving gaze finally took in the source of the Northerners' heated discussion. In the packed, damp earth near the stream, lines had been carefully drawn. Arrows and circles crossed and looped. While a part of the diagram had been smudged away by the woman's foot, the overall outline remained clear.

Daniel turned, and made his way toward Craig as quickly and as stealthily as he could.

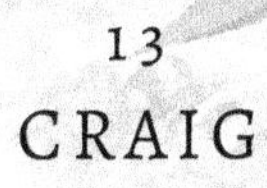

13

CRAIG

DANIEL WAS LATER than normal. Craig knew something wrong even before he arrived, and confirmed as much the second he laid eyes on his friend. Daniel was empty-handed save the fresh wounds that seeped ominous crimson onto his already stained clothes.

"What happened?"

"Northerners." Daniel adjusted his posture just slightly, and Craig realized he was no longer talking to the casual comrade he'd come to expect, but a solider in the Imperial army. "I was going for water and heard voices. Upon investigating, I was discovered and engaged. I killed one, the other—a sorcerer—got away."

"Do you think the sorcerer followed you back?" Craig glanced over his shoulder at the opening Daniel had been coming and going through.

"No, she retreated when her ally fell."

"Then we should be safe, for now." That fact was a relief, but what wasn't so relieving was enemy activity in what should be an otherwise cleared area. What place was ever truly safe in war?

"There's something else." Daniel sat next to him.

"What?"

"I don't think they were merely rogue Northerners lost or in transit between two places." The man fished around the gravel and lose rock, tapping a few stones on the floor of the cavern until he settled on one.

"And you suspect this because…?"

"I think they were scouts. Passing messages." Daniel began dragging the stone he'd selected across the rocky floor of the cavern. "They were drawing something—discussing it. It seemed important."

Craig knew what Daniel was going to say next before he said it.

"You're better with maps and direction than I am, but doesn't this look like—"

"Soricium," Craig whispered as Daniel finished his drawing. The rendering was undoubtedly rudimentary and clumsy, but the outline of the capital city was unmistakable. The inner sanctuary of Soricium, walled from the Imperial army, was surrounded by boxes that no doubt represented siege towers and weaponry. Circling around it was an outer rim that Craig knew to represent a wide perimeter of scorched earth. Even the "camp palace," a roughly crafted structure created for the comfort of head majors and Imperials, was marked.

"That's what I thought," Daniel affirmed.

"What're these?" Craig pointed at the arrows and circles Daniel had drawn last.

"I'm not sure. But I can only think they represent markers for an attack."

Craig was inclined to agree. "Things have been quiet…"

"And the Emperor just arrived," Daniel added.

That, Craig had forgotten. The Emperor had just marched back North from spending the late spring attending to matters in the Imperial capital. If the Northerners were going to launch an attack, it made the most sense that they would do it with him there, to try to cut off the head of the serpent.

"You're sure of this map?"

"I am." Daniel hesitated not at all, and Craig detected none of the false confidence that had led them astray the last time Daniel took the navigational lead.

"Then we need to let the army at Soricium know as quickly as possible." Craig bent his knee slowly and flexed his foot. The movement was easy until the muscles in his calf fully engaged, sending searing pain into his knee. He fought a grimace. Soldiers had endured worse, and he could as well. He'd had enough time to convalesce. They were in the midst of war, after all.

"I'll find some wood to splint it with," Daniel said, standing. "And another piece you can use for a walking stick."

"I'll be slow enough as it is." Craig frowned at his calf. *If they only had a cleric.*

"Better slow, alive, and well, than running to your death." There was a note of finality to Daniel's tone, one that assured Craig the matter was no longer up for discussion. How far his little foot soldier had come from the mindlessly obedient man Craig had first met when they set out together.

"I want to leave tonight."

"No." Much to his every frustration, Daniel prevented him from standing.

"If I am ever going to get back on my feet, I need to actually get back on my feet." Craig scowled at the other man.

"One more day," Daniel insisted. "It's already late in the afternoon. We won't get far and we know you're safe here. By resting now, you can move faster later and make up the time."

"I don't know if I buy that logic."

"I don't know if you have a choice." Daniel clapped him on the shoulder and stood, starting for the exit.

"Who's the lieutenant here?" Craig murmured.

"You are." He didn't need to see Daniel's face to hear the amusement at his sudden insistence on recognizing rank. In a weird way, Craig felt like he had just lost an unspoken game they'd been playing. Daniel paused near the tunnel entry, and Craig fought for something to retort with, but came up empty. "With your leave, then?" Daniel asked.

"Very well, solider." Craig twisted stubbornly, propping himself against the wall. "Though I expect the best walking stick you can find."

Daniel gave a stiff and overly formal salute. "Yes, sir!"

Craig waited until he could no longer hear Daniel's footsteps shuffling against the stone. Straightening his good leg, he eased himself back onto the ground. Laughter overtook him unexpectedly. He was wounded and one of only two men who knew of an attack launching on the Imperial army's forces. Somehow, amid it all, he found the good humor of a friend.

So perhaps everything else was slightly less impossible.

14
DANIEL

THEY MOVED FORWARD steadily through the forest. Not fast, but not painfully slow either. Craig was determined to make progress—just as Daniel was determined to keep the lieutenant's wound clean and secure.

When they stopped the first night, Craig was hissing in pain.

"Stay still or it'll hurt more," Daniel scolded. His hand wrapped around Craig's knee, trying to keep his leg in one spot so he could unravel the bandage.

"Maybe if you were a bit more gentle I wouldn't be moving so much," Craig shot back.

Daniel wanted to feel sympathy. The man had just spent the day walking on a wound that would lay up most for a week or two, at least, without proper clerical care. Unfortunately for Craig, sympathy could rarely be afforded in war.

"I'm sure it's fine. It doesn't need to be re-bandaged every day."

"In this heat? It most certainly does." Daniel continued to

unwind the remnants of his shirt that he'd cut when Craig had first fallen into the pit. He made the mental decision that today he'd sacrifice the other arm. "The springroot needs to keep being applied. Last thing you want is infection getting in there from sweat or grime."

"Have you looked at us? We're grime incarnate." Craig grinned through gritted teeth.

"You're not wrong." It was past obscene how long it had been since they last properly bathed.

"When we get to the main host and deliver this letter, and word of the impending attack… I'll put in a good word for you with the prince."

"You don't need to do that." Daniel hoped his assistance would be obvious enough to merit some kind of increase in pay.

"I most certainly do. Friends don't ignore the opportunity to lift up their friends when given the chance."

Daniel pretended to focus on the wound. The worst was almost completely healed; all that remained was the beginnings of an angry scar. *Friends.* The thought echoed in his mind. Daniel had never acquired many friends throughout the years. There was another farmhand in the neighboring field whom he would sometimes break for lunch with, a young man only a few years older than him, and one or two drinking buddies in the town center of Paca. And, of course, Willow. He'd never felt lonely, but he'd always been so focused on everything else that needed to be done that he didn't spend a lot of time sowing seeds of a social circle.

"Well, I suppose I'll repay the favor in some way."

"You already are." Craig leaned back. Daniel could see the

tension in his shoulders unraveling as the springroot seeped into his muscle. "After all, we're brothers now."

"Are we?"

"You saved my life." The man nodded down at his leg.

"I suppose you did the same." Daniel leaned back onto the ball of his right foot, taking a knee to start slicing down the arm of his shirt.

"And how is that? Certainly not leaving you for a noru cat."

"Which I still haven't forgiven you for." Daniel stopped the ripping of fabric long enough to make sure his words, and look, weren't lost.

They only served to make Craig laugh. "Sure have an odd way of showing it. Is this that infamous Eastern hospitality I keep hearing of?"

Daniel only snorted, returning to the task at hand.

"You still haven't answered the question, soldier."

"Well..." Daniel began wrapping the wound anew. "I'd certainly be lost without you here to navigate." It felt like a needed confession, and he hoped Craig would also hear the apology for getting them off track in the first place.

"Isn't that the truth?" Craig said simply.

With that, Daniel knew that his remorse was heard, and all was forgiven.

The next day, Craig led as needed, taking them deeper into the forest. Daniel didn't question how he knew the direction without map or way-finding tools. The man simply seemed to have a knack for knowing the way.

The day after that, Daniel finally questioned the matter, out of curiosity more than anything else. Craig's explanation made little sense and sounded like its own form of magic.

Something about having an internal pull toward places, his mind being able to reconstruct distances based on turns.

In the end, Daniel was left with no other option than to simply trust the man who claimed to know the right path ahead. He kept his hand on his blade and eyes at the ready. The foliage hung around them, concealing enemy movements they knew weren't too far off. Two men, in a race against the mechanizations of an entire army.

Things remained quiet until they were about a day from the capital. Then, their quiet progression ended abruptly.

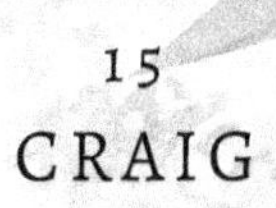

15

CRAIG

ANIEL HELD HIS **arm** across Craig's chest, stopping him mid-stride. Craig watched the other man's eyes dart around nervously, a low curse uttered under his breath. He couldn't identify any reason to be so alarmed, but that made Daniel's sudden change in pace all the more alarming.

"What is it?" Craig whispered, finally.

"Do you hear that?" Daniel breathed in reply.

"What?"

"Movement." Daniel's head tilted left, his eyes narrowing as he peered through the foliage.

Craig tried to be still, tried to hold his breath, even, but he couldn't hear anything other than the normal sounds of the forest. Had Daniel acted so strangely a few days ago, Craig might have scolded him, or brushed off his concerns. But the Easterner had since proved himself an opportunist, keenly aware of his surroundings at all times

Daniel's head snapped to attention, forward and just to the left of their projected path. Craig squinted, as if that would somehow make him hear better. Yet again nothing came to him. Just when he was about to write off the oddity as his companion's paranoia, he heard the snapping and rustling just barely at the edge of his awareness.

"I hear it too." Craig tried to keep his voice down and his ears trained on the sound, lest he loose it.

Daniel looked between Craig and the sound. Craig knew instantly what the other man was thinking.

"Scout ahead, I'll wait here, hidden." This was not the time to be proud. "But by the Mother, do not get caught and wind up dead."

"Yes, sir." Daniel pushed the messy shag of his hair away from his eyes. It almost stayed in place due to sweat and grime and the copious moisture in the air.

Craig hobbled to a nearby tree. There wasn't much shelter to be found here and the best he could do was wedge himself tightly between the large gnarls of two roots, sword at the ready. Daniel gave him one long look and proceeded to resurrect a large fern from the forest floor. He wedged one end up by Craig's head, letting it arc over him, casting him in shade.

"Be careful."

"You as well."

As Craig watched Daniel leave, the soldier suddenly looked far less green. He was certainly still rough around some edges... but those could only be buffed down with time and experience. If he kept living, kept fighting, Craig saw the makings of an exceptional swordsman. Maybe even a passable lieutenant.

Waiting was torment. By the time Daniel slunk back to his location, Craig's left hand had gone numb from where he had twisted it to keep his sword at the ready. He needn't have bothered; Daniel's expression told him everything he needed to know before the younger soldier spoke.

"It's a host, a good size, at least a full Imperial legion," Daniel reported.

"Headed in that direction?" Craig spun the world in his mind. Green blurred against green until the top suddenly lost all momentum, coming to a halt before him. He held up a finger to the east.

"Yes, it seems so," Daniel affirmed. "I didn't want to risk getting too close."

"As you shouldn't have." Craig rested his chin in his palm, struggling with their current situation. "They're marching to the Imperial Army."

"How far are we from Soricium?"

"A day and a half, perhaps," Craig murmured, thinking aloud. He mentally traversed the rugged landscape several times over. "Were any on noru cats? Or mounted on any other beast these jungles can conjure up?"

"Didn't appear so. Most were on foot." Daniel answered Craig's next question—if they were moving by treetops as Groundbreakers could do—before he could even ask it.

"At least we're well-matched there."

"How do you figure?" Daniel gave a pointed look at Craig's leg.

"We have a shot." Craig stood. "They think they have the element of surprise. They'll rest this night, traverse the rest tomorrow, strike in the dead of night the day after."

"Seems likely…"

"Then if we push, we should be able to make it to Soricium to give warning." *And deliver this Father-damned letter*, Craig added privately. But even in his moment of greatest frustration, Craig didn't give in to the idea of giving up on his mission—not after he'd come so far.

Daniel paused, looking out across the foliage. Craig wondered what insights his mind saw. He knew for certain they weren't geographical. "We still won't make it in time to give sufficient warning."

"We have to try." Craig was surprised by his friend's defeatist stance.

"I don't disagree." Daniel's voice had a somewhat faraway quality to it. "But we have to deliver the message without being there to deliver the message."

"What?" Craig wasn't a fan of riddles.

"We need to alert them to the presence of an incoming force without actually telling them the horde is on its way."

"A signal, of sorts." ~~Craig was quickly learning that Daniel's subversiveness didn't come from a desire to play games, but rather from his mental distance from the world around him. The man was utterly lost in thought, something that Craig wondered how he'd found the time to do while still keeping himself alive when they were being hunted by the noru cat.~~

"Exactly, and I think I know just the thing." Daniel stood and held out a hand to Craig. They were on the move again as Daniel spoke in a rush. "Did you ever see the ruins of old Soricium?"

Craig thought about it a long moment, recalling towering structures of stone and earth still standing stubbornly against the trees that surrounded them. They were decaying relics of bygone days, representative of something Craig had never understood—or rather, had never bothered to think about.

"I think so?"

"The crumbling towers? You had to see them, they stick out."

"Yes, yes, I know." It was true. Such construction was more Southern in style and seeing it here, in the North, was jarring. It seemed contraindicated to the tree cities curled against the trunks of the mammoth leafy guardians of the jungles.

"There should be some on the outer edge of Soricium. I remember seeing the markers of one on the way out. Can you get us to the southeast corner?"

"Maybe if we hadn't had someone directing us northward."

Daniel had the decency to look apologetic for his past stubbornness. But he also didn't dissolve into platitudes. They'd moved on from such things; the man didn't linger, and Craig respected him all the more for it.

"If we can make it down there in a day, even a day and change… We could beat the army there, get to the top of one of those towers, and light a signal."

"This relies on a lot…" Craig tried to focus on the idiocy of Daniel's plan rather than the increasing ache in his calf. "Someone seeing the signal, knowing what it means, then them being able to react, to take action—"

"It's all we have," Daniel interrupted. A shade of the man Craig had took over when he retracted his statement marginally. "Unless you can think of something better."

Craig made an attempt. But the facts were simple and damning. There wasn't a faster way they could make it to Soricium, not with his leg as it was. They certainly couldn't take on the army on their own.

"I cannot." Craig cast his lot in with the Easterner. The man had saved his life, had proven resourceful and determined. He'd done everything he could, despite Craig being willing to sacrifice him as a casualty of war, to thwart the noru cat. And his efforts had been successful so far. Craig could trust him a little bit longer. "I'll lead the way to the southeast of Soricium… and let's pray someone sees our signal, and interpret it correctly."

"Good thing Prince Baldair himself studied military signaling in his basic training."

"Pardon?"

"You didn't honestly think you were the only soldier who'd done some research on the Golden Guard, did you?" Daniel gave the smallest of smirks. He looked more like a boy playing coy than a man wielding the power of secret knowledge.

"Well, aren't you just full of surprises, Easterner?"

"Don't underestimate us farmers."

Craig agreed mutely, gritting his teeth for a moment at the pulsing pain that shot through him when a low shrub raked across his calf. When he found his breath again, something compelled him to share in that borderline conspiratorial smile. Something he was unfamiliar with, that felt curiously like kinship.

"Never again, my friend," he vowed. "Never again."

16

DANIEL

I T WAS TWILIGHT when the terrain morphed into something that could be called "familiar territory." They had trekked nearly non-stop through the blistering midday heat and chilling darkness of the forest at night. Their only pause was for a brief reprieve in the form of a restless, exhaustion-induced half-sleep.

Daniel's eyelids felt heavy and his feet dragged. He hadn't thought their trip to Soricium would be easy, but he certainly hadn't expected the pitfalls they'd encountered along the way. What could've been a break from the bloodshed had in fact become motivation to return to the relative ease of the front.

At least then he'd have a tent, and a whole host of people around him.

But the Mother worked in mysterious ways. He'd heard Westerners talk of lines of fate, and praying to the crimson sky of dawn. Daniel didn't know if he believed in all that, but certainly life was too precisely random to be perfect chance. Nothing about this journey had gone the way he'd expected.

Yet he still felt like he'd found one of the most important allies of his life in the limping man next to him.

"Not much further now," Daniel encouraged quietly. His low voice didn't come from fear of discovery as much as the inability to muster a more powerful sound.

"I'm fine."

It had been their only discussion for the past few hours: Daniel promising that it wasn't much further—even though he wasn't the one leading, even though he'd only just begun to get a vague idea of where they were. Craig continued to hear between his words, to listen to the unspoken "hang in there" injected beneath them.

This time, they were both lying.

Daniel glanced warily at Craig's leg. Blood soaked through the last of the fresh bandage. He'd need the sincere attention of a cleric, and soon. If all went well, he would have it. If all didn't go well, Craig's leg would be the least and last of their worries.

He raised his eyes to the ghostly silhouette of a long-abandoned structure. It stood against time, bleaching in the moonlight like the picked-clean bones of some unfortunate beast, corpse laying forgotten in the rocky stretch of land where the fertile Eastern plains meet the Waste. Daniel didn't know what purpose this building had once served, but now, the tombstone-shaped ruin was to become their altar of salvation.

"Okay, we're here. Now what?"

Daniel didn't blame Craig for being slightly snappish. After all, the man had just pushed himself to the limit on Daniel's hope alone… and a little white lie about Prince Baldair. Not that he should ever find that out.

"I'll scale to the top." He began searching for a good way

to get purchase upward. Hand and foot holds were plentiful, but the crumbling, weathered stone made every decision perilous. "And then I'll light a big fire."

"Using what?" Craig questioned.

"My flint."

"What will you light?" He was relentless.

Daniel's mind thought wildly. He needed something that would go up quickly. The vines that clung up the ruins were too green, too wet to catch. He needed a fire bright and hot, but more than just a flash—something that would sustain long enough to be seen.

"I'll use the remnants of my shirt as tinder…" he thought aloud.

"And what of fuel?"

Daniel looked around. His instincts first led him to a dead and hollowing tree. Plenty of firewood there. But there was no way he could get it high enough to make a signal flame, not fast enough at least.

Refusing to be thwarted, his eyes skimmed from the dead tree to where the treetops brushed against the building. Clumps of gray clung to the nooks and crannies in the stone, waving from their boughs.

"I have an idea." *A very reckless, stupid idea.*

"On an insanity scale of lying to me about knowing where you were going to trying to tangle a noru cat in tree vines by using yourself as live bait… where does this fall?"

"Closer to the latter." Daniel started for the ruins. There wasn't any more time to waste. "You go on ahead."

"Excuse me, soldier?"

Daniel heard the lieutenant's tone but wasn't backing down this time. "Go, Craig. This is going to require some running and you can't do that. Furthermore, if this doesn't work, one of us should continue on to Soricium."

Craig looked for a moment as if he would protest. But in the end, he surprised Daniel and refrained. The man held up a single finger, like a mother scolding a child. What could've been interpreted as condescending, Daniel found oddly comforting.

"Don't get yourself killed. Remember, that's an order."

"Heard, sir." Daniel was about to start his climb when he thought of one final thing. "What direction is the Northern capital?"

"That way, straight." Craig pointed through the ruins and Daniel made a note that he needed to proceed with the dead tree at his back. It was an easy enough marker.

"I'll see you there."

Craig gave one final, affirmative nod, and departed.

Daniel looked up at the ruins. It was much taller now that he stood flush at its base. He was reminded of the first time he'd stood at the foot of the great mountain the Southern capital had been built upon. He'd felt small then, too. A farm boy and his beloved hazarding the wide world to seek a better life.

This was just another mountain, albeit of a different sort, and there was only one thing you did when faced with a mountain—climb it.

One foot after the next, Daniel made his ascent. He never looked down and never spared a thought for where Craig was. He had to hope his friend would be far enough by the time the fire caught.

He was halfway to the top when his hand slipped for the first time, the stone crumbling completely under his palm. Daniel felt his body pivot backward, the anchor his hand had been using ripped from his grip. He pushed his pelvis into the stone, locked his knees and braced himself with his other arm. He allowed just enough motion to wean off the momentum, but not enough to lose his balance.

He'd chosen this particular route because it was the only patch in which the trees had not been brushing against the ruins. It was a clean path to the landings, a sort of simple stair up to the tallest point. A path completely clear of the fuel he needed.

Over time, the treetops had swayed and brushed against the crumbling stone, pulling bits and pieces free. Filling those gaps was creeping grey moss, spindly like an elderly man's beard. It clung to the stone in clumps, and was one of the few things Daniel believed would be dry enough to burn. At least, he hoped it would be.

Moving as quickly as possible, while still being mindful that every footfall could send him toppling over the edge, Daniel collected moss by the fistful. He gathered it on the lowest tier until the pile was as tall as his arm and took up a large amount of space.

Taking the ledges one at a time, he moved himself and his pile of moss upward until he finally breached the top ledge. For a breath, everything stopped.

The sky was as magnificent as it had ever been, and looked down upon him as it had always done. Daniel tilted his head back, swallowing the free currents of air that danced on the treetops. Even when things were at their darkest, the world remained. The Father still tended to his realms beyond as the Mother slept, and all the children of men waited for their return.

To the northeast, he could see the edge of Soricium. A wide ring of burnt earth encased a smaller ring of jungle, all surrounding an encampment that was a small city in its own right. He brought his eyes north, squinting at the odd peak of another ruin he'd never seen before, one located in the jungle perimeter of the siege.

Daniel made a mental note to inspect it at a later date.

He was pulled from his thoughts by movement to the northwest. Daniel saw the distinct swaying of treetops that told of enemy forces travelling on the ground beneath. The attack was close.

From up here, it seemed foolish to think that an attack on a stronghold as well-guarded as Soricium could be effective at all. But *any* attack would weaken the Empire's forces. From what Daniel had heard around camp, there weren't many forces left to scrape together for the war. The North was persistent, and if the whispers were to be believed, the Empire was running thin.

With renewed purpose, Daniel scooped up handfuls of moss, piling it high. The wind threatened to pull it away and Daniel scrambled for his sword and flint. Spearing his sword point through the center of the moss, he struck flint against steel. Sparks flew but failed to catch.

Daniel struck again, cringing at the damage the stone was doing to his blade edge. His sword needed the attention of a master smith or Firebearer the moment he returned to Soricium.

On the third strike, the moss caught.

It burned hot and bright, quickly transforming from a curling ember to a proper fire. From there, it spread quickly. Daniel dropped to the step below the top ledge and allowed his first signal to burn out.

He counted three breaths, piled on another lump, and repeated the process. Daniel burned signal fires in short succession five times. Each fire was paced specifically after the first, and he could only hope at least one of them would be seen.

Daniel squinted at the horizon, trying to see if he could discern notable movement at the camp. He waited until his patience withered and dried like the remaining moss that blew around his feet.

There's more than one way to get their attention.

His sword made a loud clang as he dug it into the stone once more. Daniel took a breath, readying himself for the final sprint. This would be the last big push. One way or another, it was all about to end.

Daniel watched as the rustling in the trees signaled the Northern force's advancement to the threshold of the burned perimeter. He waited until he was nearly certain that Craig was far enough away, waited until the last possible moment to get the army alarmed and primed.

He struck his sword with purpose, the moss catching on the first try. Daniel lifted it quickly, before the fire had much time to consume its fuel and burn the hand that held it. He turned to the deceased shell of what was once a mighty tree, its leaves already browning. If his signal fires hadn't been noticed, surely the next blaze would garner some attention.

He cast the flaming pile of moss into the tree below. Fire rained like the Mother's dawn-colored tears. It tangled in the branches and hooked on the leaves. Daniel waited just long enough to see the tree begin to catch in earnest, moss and flame alike clinging to what would be the largest pyre any single person could hope to make.

Then, in the wake of crackling flame already hot on the wind, he set to running.

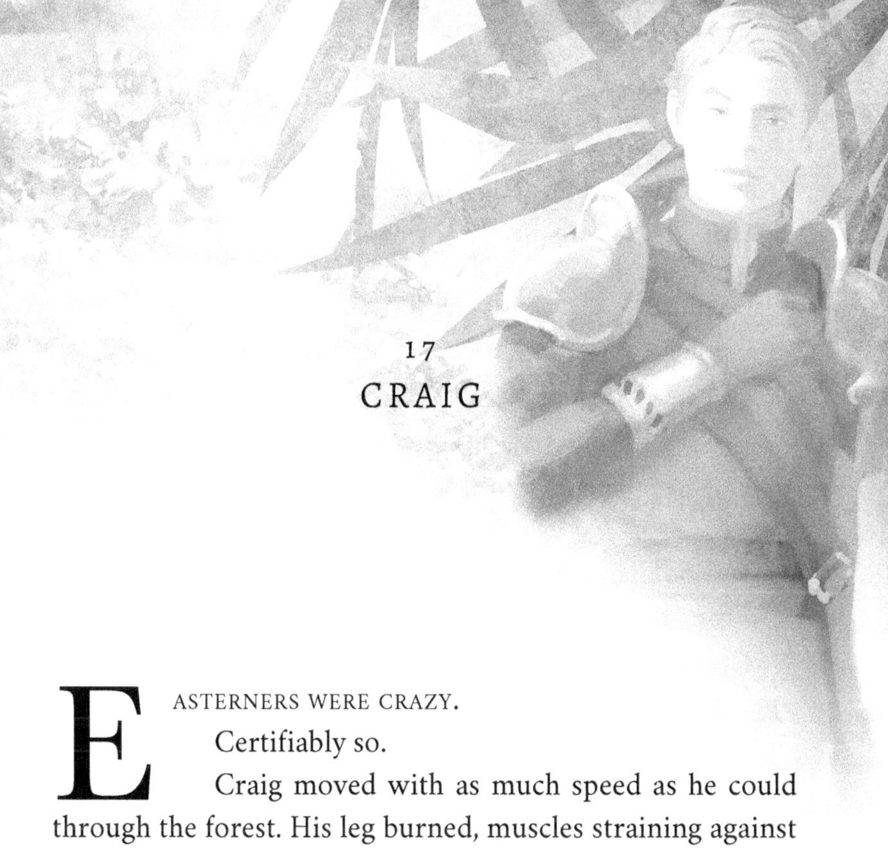

17

CRAIG

EASTERNERS WERE CRAZY.

Certifiably so.

Craig moved with as much speed as he could through the forest. His leg burned, muscles straining against the bandages. He could feel the start of blood beginning to pool in the sole of his shoe.

It didn't take a cleric to figure out what would happen if he continued as he was. The tender tissue that had been steadily repairing with time was being ripped open anew. Now it was being torn in different ways—ways likely beyond mending.

Craig placed a hand on his waist where the letter was, and picked up his pace to a run.

The pain made him clench his teeth until his jaw ached. Everything or nothing—this was his test. He'd heard the older soldiers speak of defining moments, times when everything else had been scraped away and they discovered the mettle they were made of underneath it all.

Jax had his tumultuous past and unprecedented redemption with Prince Baldair.

Erion had been one of the few to ever best the boy prince in combat.

Raylynn had saved the prince's life in the Waste.

This would be his moment. He would shine for the prince and prove his worth. This would be the day when everything changed for him, when the nothing and no one boy from a small Southern town would finally find his purpose.

Behind him, the jungle was erupting in flames.

From his left, he heard breaking branches and rustling leaves. Craig dug his good heel hard into the soft earth to spin in place. His sword rang out against the scabbard as he drew it, holding it at the ready to meet whatever enemy the fire had drawn forth.

The moment Craig saw movement he lunged, sword point targeted to kill. But by the grace of the moon shifting in the trees and reflected flames, he saw a familiar set of eyes and shifted at the last moment.

Daniel ducked as well, and the point of the sword stuck into the tree right by his shoulder. He straightened some distance away, sparing a glance for the weapon that had been aimed, mere seconds ago, at his face.

"Hello to you too."

"I thought you were an enemy." Craig wiggled the blade free. When it popped from the bark he had to take a step to catch his balance. Fire shot up from his calf, straight into his neck. It was easier if he kept moving. Moving brought numbness, and numbness was necessary to survive.

"Last I saw from above, they were still slightly north." Daniel turned in the wrong direction, to look at some unseen foe. Craig saw a long gash running across the man's chin, but he looked overall unscathed.

"Who knows where they'll come from when you're burning down half the jungle." Craig's voice was half a shout as he started to run again. The volume helped mask the pain, and there was really no point in being subtle any longer.

"Just the one spot is burning." Daniel had the audacity to sound amused.

The banter was welcome, even if Craig couldn't reply any longer; if he opened his mouth he'd be howling in agony. So he kept focused on the task at hand—getting himself to Soricium.

As they ran, the sounds of battle began to rise over the noise of leaves and trees bending and snapping around them. Fire was behind them, and now fire was before them. The Imperial Firebearers were already acting in response to the attack.

Though he knew it would look more like a grimace than a smile, Craig couldn't stop his mouth from turning upward in relief. He'd never smiled running into battle before, but something about tonight was different. Pain numbed his body, leaving only his mind, his training, and his instinct.

They burst through the trees into the blackened, burned perimeter that surrounded Soricium—out of the darkness of the forest and into the flames of the Mother herself.

Imperial steel clashed against Northern wavy blades. The Black Legion held a wall of flame that kept out the majority of the infantry, but the strongest Groundbreakers and Northerners, skin coated in a green repellant, barreled through. Craig's eyes scanned the field, knowing he only had a split second to take in the state of things before—

He dodged to the side, spinning his blade in his palm and

using the momentum to twist and bring it behind him in a back-handed slash.

It rang out against a Northern sword. The woman was wrapped tightly underneath armor made of nearly impenetrable tree bark, the same that coated the giants of the forest. She snarled at the parry and went for another attack.

Her breaths were notes, her footsteps beats, and the sword swings kept tempo to a song Craig tried his best to hear. Raylynn had told him of the song of the sword, the melody of battle. She'd spoken of it as though it were some spiritual experience, and not practical combat methodology. Craig had hung on her every word. And even if he may not have fully understood it… he trusted her.

He slid his sword from the woman's gut and she collapsed before him. His eyes scanned the area immediately surrounding him, looking for an Easterner with a pommel of gold and a tunic with ripped-off arms. He found gold, but not in the way he'd been expecting.

She was unmistakable, appearing like a vision from the Mother. Raylynn's hair haloed around her, moving as if underwater in the shifting firelight. She was surrounded, ten on her at once, but fought with the same ease as if she were in the dueling ring.

The woman was like water, fluid, effortless, and apparently immune to the swings of a sword as the steel almost magically ducked and dipped around her.

It was time for Craig to prove himself to the guard. And to his teacher.

Craig sprinted in Raylynn's direction, engaging two Northerners along the way. The third posed the greatest threat as his sword chipped off a patch of exposed neck, the warrior carrying on with the same determined brutality they had engaged him with. *Groundbreaker*. Craig cursed his luck.

The man attacked with a short sword, aiming for the open spot under Craig's arm as he swung into his own attack. In attempts to dodge, Craig did a clumsy bit of footwork, his leg almost failing him. He was not properly outfitted for a fight. Light leather armor was designed to offer minimal protection, just enough to flee as he made his ride through the forest to deliver the letter. He had dressed for speed, not combat. Now he was wishing he'd known better.

By the time Craig's sword point found its way into the man's eye, he was sporting a new gash on his arm. It was a small price to pay. Craig looked back to Raylynn, but caught only the briefest glimpse before a new wall of fire sparked in front of him.

Instinctually, he raised his hands to cover his face, but it did little to shield him from the wave of heat that nearly knocked him off his feet.

"Let me through!" he shouted hopelessly, for any Black Legion sorcerers who might be around to hear. "I must get through!"

"She needs you," a voice said, close enough that Craig almost jumped from his skin and gouged out the speaker's gut.

The young woman was all hard, defined angles, with eyes sharp enough to slice a man's skin and soul in a single glance. She looked as resolute as the trees that pillared the landscape behind her, but as alive as the fire that burned before her. She had the dark hair and tanned skin of a Westerner, but this close to the fire, she seemed to glow with magic itself.

"Who—"

"Raylynn Westwind, I'm here to help you get to her." The woman was swathed in black, but didn't bear the usual broken moon sigil of a Black Legion sorcerer. She also wore an odd formation of leather armor, lacquered with a material unfamiliar to Craig.

"Are you Imperial?" Her garb was utterly foreign and didn't seem to belong to either group.

There was a slight pause. The fire before him seemed to waver, and Craig wondered if he imagined the decrease in heat.

"I am not," she whispered. "I am of Yargen."

Craig held out his sword and she stared down the edge of the blade.

"I am not your enemy, Craig Youngly. And even if I was, you cannot kill me." There was a kind of sorrow in her words. "I will only die when my task is complete."

"Who are you?" He wanted to shout but could only whisper; he had no idea how she'd heard him over the sounds of the battle raging around them.

"I've had many names." The woman brought her eyes back to the fire, focusing intently on it. "Now… Go."

She held up her hand and the flames parted and arched, creating a tunnel through the conflagration. Craig stared at the strange woman for one more long moment before turning to run. His leg was beginning to fail him, and if it was going to give out and turn him into meat for someone's blade, he would spend the last of his strength defending his teacher and working toward the one thing in his meager life he'd ever wanted.

The flames closed behind him, and the woman vanished from his sight as mysteriously as she'd appeared.

Craig's eyes landed on Raylynn. She was struggling, jumping over bodies she'd no doubt cut down. *Where were Jax and the rest of the batallion? Why was she alone?* Questions rose, though their answers didn't matter. The only thing that mattered was jumping into the fray.

"Raylynn!" Craig shouted, announcing his presence.

The whirlwind of sword strikes around the woman quieted briefly enough to acknowledge his presence. Her eyebrows knitted and Raylynn transformed into ire incarnate.

"Where have you been?" Anger made her even more deadly, and she stormed over to him, cutting down three on the way.

"Trying to—why are you here?" Questions jumbled together and fell clumsily from his lips.

"Looking for you!" She wasn't too busy protecting herself to clock him upside the head, it would seem.

Raylynn Westwind, sword major, Golden Guard member, one of the best fighters in the entire world, had gone off looking for him? It made no sense, and his puzzlement must have shown on his face.

"You idiot." She rolled her eyes. "Later. For now, just don't die."

Craig's leg howled in pain, but it didn't drown out the song in his heart, nor the harmony it made as he fought alongside his mentor.

HE'D LOST CRAIG in the fray. For an exhausted man with one gimp leg and a stink that left a near-visible trail through the air, the fact was damn near impressive.

Daniel gave one more sweep of the battlefield, but couldn't distinguish his Southerner from any of the other Imperialists amid the attack. Which meant there was only one thing left for him to do. His fingers closed around the pommel of his sword.

There was a certain serenity that could be found in the vibration of steel through the bones in his arm. It shot straight between his ears and buzzed against his thoughts. Daniel didn't thrive off the field as some did; his sword was simply a means to an end. But that end was Willow—their future—and he fought for everything they would need to be comfortable for the rest of their lives.

His sword punctured the chest of the first enemy that descended on him, the first of many blood taxes he'd collect before the night was through.

Daniel withdrew his sword with a *swish* through the air. Blood arced off in rivulets, spattering the ground and the face of two more Northerners advancing on him. *Marked for death*, he thought grimly.

A woman lunged for him and Daniel knew instantly she was the more skilled of the two. Her bladework was impeccable, and she fought with a fearlessness that only came from well-earned confidence. Daniel danced around the dual blades with all the swiftness he still possessed.

There was no shame in admitting when you were bested in battle. In fact, that was how most soldiers stayed alive for so long, he'd discovered. Heroes died. Strategists survived.

Step by step, blow by blow, Daniel spun and ducked around his advancing opponents. With a side shuffle, he could work his way around to see the rest of the fray. Imperial soldiers were being divided into two core groups. Which meant…

Daniel shifted from defense to offense. Catching the woman's blade with the pommel of his sword, he pushed off and in, engaging her more closely than he had before. The woman had height on him, so Daniel knew that close proximity would make her struggle.

A familiar rumble rose up from the inner forest, closest to Soricium on the burnt stretch. Daniel began running in its direction. The two he'd been fending off were on him with a shout and a snarl. At the last moment, he banked right.

The cavalry burst through the tree line and into the field between the two groups of infantry. Daniel cleared the first horse with a jump and roll. The two better soldiers at his heels were lost to the hooves and poles of the mounted soldiers.

At the front of the line, sword in hand, white cape billowing behind him in the firelight, was the man Daniel and Craig had been seeking since the start. The Golden Prince, youngest son of the Empire, Prince Baldair led the charge with a shout: "Down and around, cut them off at the woods!"

The prince made some motions corresponding with his orders, punctuating them all with a quick stab of his sword at some unfortunate soul below.

"Misha, take your group and survey the signal we spotted—"

My signal, Daniel realized.

"—Bring extras to engage the fray there."

"Sir, my prince," Daniel hastily corrected, "there is no fray where the signal was set."

The prince looked around a moment, confounded by the source of the voice. His eyes swept over Daniel twice until, on the third pass, Daniel gave a stiff salute. It was the first time royalty so much as breathed in his direction, and he did not want to ruin his first impression… if he hadn't already done so by going rogue and setting the forest on fire.

"Who are you?" the prince asked.

"Daniel Taffl, sir. Swords, under Major Raylynn, sir."

"Major Raylynn?" Prince Baldair spurred his horse over to Daniel. "What are you doing here? Did you desert your post? What news of Raylynn?" The prince asked all his questions in a single breath, leaving Daniel to filter out what was the most important among them.

Daniel decided to focus on the one thing that made the prince's questioning voice sound truly strained. "When I left at her orders, sir, Major Raylynn was well. She sent Craig Youngly and me on a mission to deliver a letter to you.

During this time, we discovered news of this attack. I sent the signal to warn the main host, then set the forest ablaze...for good measure, sir."

He had to shout over the sounds of swords clashing and trees crackling, but the prince seemed to focus only on what Daniel had to say, allowing the other cavalry to run protection for a moment. With Daniel's tidy speech concluded, the prince permitted himself a brief survey of his surrounds before suddenly snapping back to Daniel.

"You were the one who gave the signal?"

"I was." Daniel swallowed hard. His throat had gone to dust.

The prince's silence ticked away the longest seconds of Daniel's life. When the golden-haired man spoke again, it was with a grin.

"Stay with me, Daniel. You did say your name was Daniel, right?"

He nodded, disbelieving.

"Stay with me then through this fray. I wish to speak to you, but first, we must do battle."

The prince was a little too gleeful as he twirled his sword through the night air. Daniel redrew his blade as well, adding the slightest flourish. He would not see the royal outdone, but if he was fighting next to the Golden Prince himself, he could afford a bit of flair.

The two re-joined the fray as dawn broke over the treetops.

19

CRAIG

A STEAMING CUP of tea was placed between his palms in a manner that indicated there was no room for discussion on the matter. Unlike the others he'd choked down at the cleric's insistence, there was no herbal tang to sizzle his nose. Craig looked up, still in an exhausted daze.

"Just tea." Raylynn sat on a bench opposite his own. "Thought you could use something straight to wash down all those potions."

"Thank you." Craig lifted the cup to his lips tiredly and took a long drink. It barely had any taste at all—was likely nothing more than jungle leaves steeped in a boiling pot. But at war, the shack they were in was a palace, the clerics making due with rudimentary tinctures were alchemists, and water perfumed with mysterious greens was tea.

"A noru cat, huh?" Raylynn arched her eyebrows, referencing Craig's explanation of the events that had led him back to Soricium.

"That was not my fault."

"You were the highest in command," she chastised. "Everything is your fault." Raylynn gave a soft laugh as the words hit Craig square in the chest, deflating his sails. "But I think, given the wound you endured for it... Well, the Mother has already offered her punishment for your foolishness."

He knew all was forgiven then, and laid to rest his fears of losing his chance at a golden bracer. Craig stared at his leg, slowly being bandaged in the cleanest looking gauze he'd ever seen—though his main point of reference was Daniel's soiled shirt.

Daniel.

"Did you see Daniel on the field?" Craig asked suddenly.

"I did not." Raylynn's mouth set into a grim line. She no more liked the idea of losing Daniel than he did; the war needed his sword.

"Well, then..." Craig floundered for words. "I suppose—" He was interrupted by the doors opening, and fate taking that as its cue to decide for him on what needed to be done.

Daniel looked as relieved to see Craig as he was Daniel. The lieutenant instinctually moved to get to his feet.

"Stay down," the cleric scolded.

"Glad to see you made it," Daniel said after a moment, starting for the small corner of bench not occupied by Craig's sprawling form.

"No need to stand," said another voice, clearly mistaking Craig's instinct to rise for the sake of greeting Daniel as protocol in the face of royalty.

Craig was always a little dumbstruck in the presence of the prince. He'd met Baldair before, a few times actually, around Raylynn. But there was something about seeing him in the flesh, and right in front of him, that gave Craig rightful pause. The Golden Prince could make the hovel of haphazard walls and uneven ceiling look positively regal.

"Sir." Craig stood as straight as possible.

"Just Baldair is fine." The prince waved away the formality. "I've seen you with Ray enough times to know that you're one of her favorites."

The prince's eyes strayed to the lounging figure of the woman herself. Raylynn, all limbs, sprawled across the benches and tables like a spool of silk tossed to the wind and left to unravel. She gave him a coy smile that was eagerly returned.

"What mischief have you made?" Baldair asked her, taking one notable step into her personal space. There was that odd familiarity between the two of them, the bane of every eligible bachelorette in the Empire.

"This mischief is not my doing, but Jax's." The elegant curve of her mouth bent uncomfortably into a frown. "Mischief that almost got my protégé killed."

"Protégé?"

Raylynn motioned to Craig, whose chest nearly burst from pride.

"Tell Jax to play with his own toys, and stay away from mine," Raylynn finished. Craig's ego was instantly put back in check.

The mention of the sorcerer brought Craig's hand to his side in a panic. Through it all, the fold of leather he'd tied to his chest had remained. Craig shifted and shuffled, wiggling it free. Carefully, he unfolded it and presented the still-sealed missive to the prince.

"Baldair—" Daniel must have rubbed off on him, as it was suddenly hard to not use formalities. "—My prince, I was tasked with bringing this to you."

The prince crossed the narrow room in three wide steps. With a shake of his head Craig felt wasn't directed at him, he set to opening the letter. Whatever it contained was not very long, as he'd read it twice in a few seconds.

"Really?" The prince looked back to Raylynn, who couldn't seem to contain her laughter.

"Well, it went a bit south." She spoke through giggles. "But it would have been amusing."

"Why do I keep you both in my Guard?" Baldair folded the paper and threw it onto a far table where it did a small spin, half the folds coming undone.

"Truly a good question, prince."

"It wasn't a total loss." Baldair turned to Daniel and, in that moment, Craig saw the look of pride and interest he'd been wanting to see for years... directed at another soldier. "We knew about that attack, thanks to you, Daniel."

"It was nothing, sir."

"Baldair," the prince corrected. Craig aimed a side-eye at his friend that went unnoticed. Really, the man was stubborn if he was clinging to titles after the prince had instructed him otherwise. "And it *was* something. Father estimated the casualties could've been double if they'd caught us in our beds."

"What happened?" Raylynn's brow knitted the way it always did when she was presented with a puzzle.

Baldair began to recount the small gap in the story Craig had left out. He could've set off that signal fire if it weren't for his leg. He could've been the one to warn the army.

It should have been me.

"His swordsmanship shows that same cleverness," Raylynn praised brightly, as though he or Daniel weren't even in the room.

"I saw that first hand in the scuffle earlier."

This couldn't be happening. Craig had been eager to take this mission because he'd wanted the opportunity to shine before the prince. He had taken Daniel to prevent him further earning Raylynn's admiration. Now, he'd done the opposite on all counts.

"Though, I would like to see more of this clever swordsmanship." The prince turned to Daniel; Craig may as well have not even existed. "Come to the training grounds with me?"

"You're relentless," Raylynn groaned. "Did we not just finish a battle?"

"Perfect time to test the true strength of a metal is when it would be at its most brittle."

"Who did you steal that line from?" Raylynn stood without being asked, following Daniel's lead.

"I thought of it myself."

"You can't think yourself out of a burlap sack." There were certain things only Raylynn could get away with when it came to the prince.

"Terribly harsh, Ray. Is that any way to treat me after we've been apart for so long?" Baldair's laughter followed him out the door, Raylynn close behind.

Daniel lingered a moment, hovering in the doorframe. His lips parted briefly.

Craig pointedly looked away from him. When he finally had the courage to bring his eyes back, it was to the shutting of the door—closing not just on the now empty room, but on his singular dream and aspiration.

20

DANIEL

CRAIG HAD BEEN avoiding him, of that much he was certain.

The man was transparent as glass and as easy to read as a children's primer. Daniel knew from the moment Baldair had walked in singing his praises that it was only a matter of time until Craig began to sting. "A matter of time" proved a mere instant, the sting far more dire than what plagued his injured leg.

It had been almost a month since their return to Soricium. Raylynn "couldn't be bothered" to go back and find her battalion, putting every faith in her second to lead in her stead. For a woman who cared about so little, the fact that she would go out of her way to ride through the jungle alone, taking the most logical route in search of Craig and Daniel, spoke volumes.

The fact said something to Craig as well, because Raylynn was the only one who could seem to find him. Daniel would ask her, whenever their paths crossed, but by the time he arrived at the spot she claimed to have last seen

Craig, the man would have vanished. He wouldn't be surprised if it was by design. Daniel had no idea how he'd curried any favor with Raylynn, but he well knew that favor didn't extend over Craig's.

The day before they were to return to the South, Daniel set out to scour the camp on his own. If he would have any chance of hunting Craig down, he'd need to do it himself. And, while he would usually respect a person's wishes at all costs—and especially a superior's wishes—this was one time he needed a moment, even if a moment wasn't something Craig wanted to give.

Daniel finally found the blonde haired man helping load carts for the few noble sick who would be transported back to better care in the Southern Capital. It was a luxury not everyone had earned, or could afford.

"Your leg looks better." Daniel appreciated the startle Craig gave at his voice. It affirmed two things: that he had, indeed, been avoiding him, and that Craig had no idea Daniel set out to hunt him down this morning.

Craig turned, and it was no surprise where his gaze fell. "Your arm, too."

Daniel touched the golden band that circled his forearm. "Baldair gave it to me last night."

"I heard." Craig hauled a particularly heavy basket onto the cart. "You've dropped 'sir' and 'prince,' I see."

"Walk with me?" Daniel wanted to be straightforward before tensions could escalate to outright hostilities.

"I'm fairly busy here," Craig mumbled.

Daniel looked purposefully down at the one sack Craig had left to load. When the other man didn't move, he lifted it with a small sigh, throwing it onto the cart. Clerical supplies were surprisingly heavy.

"Looks like you just finished up."

Craig stared at him, searching, internal debate clear across his face. "Fine. What is it?"

"Raylynn tells me that after you return to the Capital for the Festival of the Sun, you won't be marching on another tour?" Daniel relayed the one bit of information Raylynn had divulged—the part that seemed most pertinent to the situation.

"I'm done with fighting." Craig shrugged as if that would help sell a lie so poorly constructed, it barely rang with the slightest peel of truth. "I'll return home, become a hunter."

"A hunter," Daniel repeated with marked amusement.

"What's so funny?"

"Given your showing with the noru cat, I find it difficult to imagine you hunting anything at all."

"That is hardly a good example." Craig folded his arms over his chest and Daniel gave up on the subject before he risked truly upsetting his companion.

"I was hoping you'd come on another tour."

After a long stretch of silence, Craig rose to the bait. "And why is that?"

"Because it would be a shame for a member of the Golden Guard not to march with the rest of us." Craig grew still, like a fawn suddenly aware of a predator lurking nearby.

"What are you talking about?"

"You heard I'd been made a member of the guard... but you didn't seem to hear that the membership was conditional." Daniel reached into the satchel he wore slung over his shoulder and retrieved a second bracer nearly identical to the one he currently wore on his wrist.

Craig's face traversed the spectrum of emotions.

Surprise, desire, appreciation, skepticism, and then—what Daniel had expected least—anger.

"I don't want your charity."

"This isn't charity. You earned it," Daniel insisted. He kept talking before Craig could get in another self-deprecating word. "Raylynn insisted too."

The mention of his mentor soothed Craig some. "She did?"

"She did. And Baldair was enthusiastic as well. He even said, 'Daniel and Craig, sounds good together, like its own name.'" Daniel laughed at the thought.

"Why did you do this?" Craig's hands half-hovered in the air. Daniel knew he was just about ready to accept his new role, but hesitation lingered.

"Why?" He thought it would've been obvious. "Because we both know I'd be lost without you. If I get sent out on a mission, how the hell will I ever find my way?"

"So I'm to be your navigator?" Craig's grin gave away that his words were not, in reality, rooted in ire.

"Because I may have started to enjoy your company?"

"May have?" It wasn't good enough either.

"Because I'm told this guard is all about brotherhood. And are you not my brother?"

That did it.

Craig extended his forearm and Daniel twisted his wrist into the golden bracer. "And since you are indeed the brother I was never born with, I wanted to see your dream come to pass."

Craig slowly pulled his arm to his chest, running his hands over the bracer now extended from wrist nearly to elbow. Daniel noticed his reverence for the token, and felt reaffirmed in his decision. Craig would be a good addition to the guard, that he knew. No one else in the army wanted it more than him.

"Well, now that my dream has come to pass... we shall see to yours."

"And what dream is that?" They resumed their walk back toward the center of camp.

"Your position in the castle—which you are all but assured now." Craig tapped his bracer. "And your Willow, married and fat with your children."

Daniel laughed. "If she so chooses to bestow children on me, then yes."

"And you know, through it all, Uncle Craig will be there to help."

"Uncle Craig?" Daniel repeated, amused.

"Is that not what a brother is to his brother's children?"

"You are right, indeed," Daniel agreed with a small smile.

"Trust me, I'll always know the way." Craig threw his arm around Daniel's shoulder and the two walked toward the Camp Palace.

Daniel turned his eyes skyward, toward the infinite stretch of blue above them. He wondered if Willow looked up at the same sky, if she longed for him as he did for her. He would find out soon enough.

For the first time, Daniel felt like his life was on course for far greater things than a farmer's son ever could have hoped.

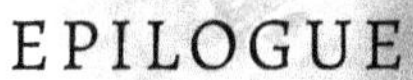

EPILOGUE

Craig stared out the window listlessly. War had followed them from the North. The army had returned with all the fanfare and celebration one could expect, hollow victors waving banners without meaning.

Soricium still had not fallen. Despite the Emperor's bold claims, none of them had any reason to believe the conflict would end before winter was over. Time and again, the Northerners proved nothing if not resourceful, determined, and cunning.

In the fading light of the sun, he could still see the smoldering remains of a good portion of the Southern Capital. A few determined Northerners had done much damage, and not just to the capital. If there was any hope of integrating them with the South, it had been lost with this attack.

And then, there were the even stranger circumstances that had thwarted them.

Craig turned his eyes to a patch of town at the apex of it

all. There, the buildings had been blown to gravel. A windstorm in the capital, a vortex of sound and gale. Craig shuddered at the mere thought of such sorcery.

The door to the sitting room opened and Craig's attention pulled away from the destruction to a familiar silhouette.

"Baldair is looking for you," Raylynn announced.

"For what?" he asked, though he was already moving toward the door.

"Who knows with him anymore." Raylynn shrugged. "He seems genuinely concerned for Prince Aldrik's play thing?"

Craig had always noted that Raylynn never dropped the elder prince's title. For all her brazenness and lack of care, she remained true to decorum for only three: the Emperor, the Crown Prince, and the Lord of the West.

"The girl who made the windstorm?" Craig remembered Baldair mentioning the sport he'd been having at his elder brother's expense, but it seemed par for the course for the two of them—nothing of note.

At least, nothing of note until the word "Windwalker" entered the conversation.

"He's in his room."

Craig never thought he would've been given easy access to the Imperial quarters of the palace. But with the golden cuff on his arm, nothing was off-limits. Still, the gilded splendor of the palace never lost its shine with Craig.

Baldair was just where Raylynn said he'd be, pacing around the billiards table in the sitting area of his personal chamber. His crown—a simple golden circlet—had been discarded haphazardly along with his ceremonial cape. There was a rare knit to the prince's brow.

"You wanted to see me?"

"Ah, yes, Craig…" Baldair seemed slow to recollect why he had summoned his most recent addition to the Guard. "I have a task for you."

"Yes?"

"I need you to guard the prisoner. The girl, Vhalla Yarl."

"The one from last night…?" Craig asked hesitantly. "She's a sorcerer, shouldn't Jax—"

"No." Baldair shook his head. "Jax draws too much attention just by breathing. It must be you. But take off your bracer. Don't let her know of your association with me just yet."

"Why not?" There were forces at play here beyond Craig's understanding—that much was becoming more apparent by the second.

"I put her in this situation." Baldair ran a hand through his hair. His strained tone prevented further inquiry, despite Craig's burning desire for details. "I don't think she'll want anyone associated with me."

"Bracer will be removed, then."

"Go to her promptly. She'll be in need of new guards soon enough."

"What happened to her last ones?"

"A fate you won't have to worry about." Baldair smiled sadly, but left his cryptic answer lingering.

"One thing…" A thought crossed Craig's mind that couldn't be put aside once it had jumped to the forefront of his thoughts. "I'd like Daniel to be stationed with me."

"I was going to suggest it, had you not brought it up."

That was one of the many things Craig appreciated about the prince—his attentiveness to his loyal subjects.

"How is he handling things?"

"Not well." Craig had been having a hard time getting the man to say anything the past few days.

"I'm not surprised." Baldair sighed heavily. "So many things need fixing... Maybe we should stop breaking them for while."

The statement was said mostly to himself, in a moment that proved Baldair was several times the man anyone regularly gave him credit for.

"I'll go find him now." Craig dismissed himself.

Daniel was out by the training field. He'd taken to scribbling in a notebook ever since Willow had left, but he never let anyone else see what he wrote, not even Craig. As expected, the leather book snapped shut the moment Craig approached.

"We have a job," Craig said before Daniel could send him away.

Daniel merely blinked at him.

"I know you're still stinging from Willow." At the mention of the woman's name, Daniel glanced askance. It was a far improved reaction than the inconsolable man he'd been a few weeks ago after the woman broke his heart. "But there's a person. She needs our help." He may have been exaggerating a bit, but the heavier words seemed to carry the desired weight. At the very least, Craig hoped this mission would once more imbue his friend with a sense of purpose. Daniel had seemed lost since he no longer had a wife to fight for and a home to build.

"Who?" Daniel asked softly.

"Her name is Vhalla Yarl, and Baldair has informed me that we are to protect her."

Daniel was still and silent, processing in his own reticent way. Finally he stood, rising with the wind up the mountain.

It was the first moment in recent memory that he seemed to stand fully upright—to fully embody himself.

"Then protect her we shall."

I hope you loved the Golden Guard trilogy as much as I loved writing it! If you have a spare moment, please consider leaving an honest review on any of the books on your retailer of choice. It doesn't have to be long—one sentence or two. But it really helps authors!

There's more to the world of Air Awakens

Continue reading to learn more...

DISCOVER MORE FROM ELISE KOVA

Epic Fantasy.
Adventure.
Magic.
Deep Emotions.

See all books at:

http://EliseKova.com/books

VORTEX VISIONS

A fantasy epic. Go on an adventure across place and time.

Get your copy: https://elisekova.com/vortex-visions-air-awakens-vortex-chronicles-1/

Trained to take the throne. Born to save the world.

A PRINCESS...

Vi Solaris has grown up far from home, sequestered, and trained to one day be Empress. The two things she wants most? Freedom and magic. Vi has neither.

That is until her powers manifest, dangerous and forbidden.

A POWER...

Now, alongside her royal studies, she trains in secret with a mysterious sorcerer from a far-away land. From his pointed ears to enchanting eyes, he's nothing like anyone she's ever met before. She should fear him, but she finds herself more and more entranced by the day.

Now, she's bound to him along with the fate of a dying world.

A CHOICE...

Her inability to control her magic might cost her the throne. Her captivity might prevent her from thwarting the assassins out to kill her. The Empire is faltering from political infighting and a deadly plague. Vi must make the hardest choice of her life:

Play by the rules and claim her throne. Or, break them for a magic she was never supposed to have.

Fans of Throne of Glass, Red Queen, Oath Taker, and Furyborn will love this young adult, epic fantasy world filled with elemental magic, friendships as deep as blood, shocking twists, thrilling adventures, and slow-burn romance.

A TRIAL OF SORCERERS

The sorcerer games have begun.

Get your copy: https://elisekova.com/a-trial-of-sorcerers/

Ice is in her blood.

Eighteen-year-old Waterrunner Eira Landan lives her life in the shadows - the shadow of her older brother, of her magic's whispers, and of the person she accidentally killed. She's the most unwanted apprentice in the Tower of Sorcerers until the day she decides to step out and compete for a spot in the Tournament of Five Kingdoms.

Pitted against the best sorcerers in the Empire, Eira fights to be one of four champions. Excelling in the trials has its rewards. She's invited to the royal court with the "Prince of the Tower," discovers her rare talent for forbidden magic, and at midnight, Eira secretly meets with a handsome elfin ambassador.

But, Eira soon learns, no reward is without risk. As she comes into the spotlight, so too do the skeletons of a past she hadn't even realized was haunting her.

Eira went into the trials ready for a fight. Ready to win. She wasn't ready for what it would cost her. No one expected the candidates might not make it out with their lives.

A Trial of Sorcerers is the first book in a brand new, young adult, epic fantasy for readers who love stories involving: sorcerer competitions, slow-burn romance, adventures to distant lands, and elemental magic.

powerful sorcerers of them all--the Crown Prince Aldrik--she
finds herself enticed into his world. Now she must decide her
future: Embrace her sorcery and leave the life she's known, or
eradicate her magic and remain as she's always been. And with
powerful forces lurking in the shadows, Vhalla's indecision could
cost her more than she ever imagined.

**Get ready for an epic fantasy, filled with romance and
adventure, in Air Awakens, the first book in a completed five
book series. Are you ready? Scroll up and click buy now to see
why readers love the Air Awakens series!**

ABOUT THE AUTHOR:
ELISE KOVA

View a full list of Elise Kova's novels on Amazon here: http://author.to/EliseKova

ELISE KOVA is a USA Today bestselling author. She enjoys telling stories of fantasy worlds filled with magic and deep emotions. She lives in Florida and, when not writing, can be found playing video games, drawing, chatting with readers on social media, or daydreaming about her next story.

She invites readers to get first looks, giveaways, and more by subscribing to her newsletter at: http://elisekova.com/ subscribe

Visit her on the web at:
http://elisekova.com/
https://www.tiktok.com/@elisekova
https://www.facebook.com/AuthorEliseKova/
https://www.instagram.com/elise.kova/